"If you need taking care of, I'm the one to do it.

This pregnancy is as much my responsibility as yours. I'm the guy who should be your roommate."

Stacy touched her still-flat abdomen, keenly aware of what lay inside. Part of her longed to lean against Cole and yield to his guardian instincts, but she'd learned caution, the hard way. "One disastrous mistake per relationship is the legal limit. And we used ours when we did this."

"Why would living together be a mistake?" he pressed.

"Because I'm vulnerable," she said. "Have you ever fallen in love?"

He frowned. "Define falling in love?"

Oh, for pity's sake! "If you ever do, you won't have to ask. It will sweep away everything else like a wildfire."

Dear Reader,

While visiting a friend, I was delighted to meet her daughter-in-law, a nurse who's an approved egg donor and who generously answered my questions. What is the process? What are the pitfalls? Why would she, as the married mother of two children, choose to do this?

In addition to being impressed by her generosity, I was startled to learn that egg donors have to be very careful during the rest of the cycle. The harvesting process often misses some eggs, and if they become pregnant, they could find themselves carrying multiple babies.

Naturally, that implied a story line. Developing it proved a challenging process, and I hope you enjoy the results.

Nurse Stacy appeared as a secondary character in *The M.D.'s Secret Daughter,* in which she had a crush on Dr. Zack Sargent. Cole was introduced in the same book and had a few run-ins with Zack over hospital issues.

Moving them to center stage required deepening and expanding their characters. Cole especially surprised me. Going inside his head proved a journey into a rather unusual character. In my ninety earlier novels, I don't believe I've ever created a hero like him. But then, I don't feel as if I create my characters—rather, they reveal themselves to me.

Welcome to Cole and Stacy's story!

Best,

Jacqueline Diamond

The Baby Jackpot

Jacqueline Diamond

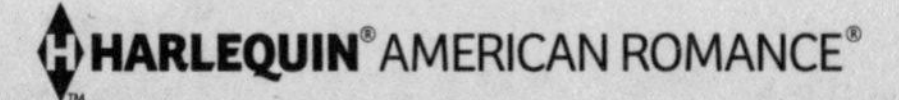

ISBN-13: 978-0-373-75447-2

THE BABY JACKPOT

This edition published by arrangement with Harlequin Books S.A.

For questions and comments about the quality of this book, please contact us at CustomerService@Harlequin.com.

Printed in U.S.A.

ABOUT THE AUTHOR

The author of ninety romances, mysteries, Regencies and paranormals, Jacqueline Diamond lives in Orange County, California, with her husband of more than thirty years. Writing about a fertility program at a medical center draws on Jackie's long-standing interest in medicine, which began when her father, then the only doctor in the small Texas town of Menard, delivered her at home. You can learn more about Jackie and the Safe Harbor Medical series at www.jacquelinediamond.com.

Books by Jacqueline Diamond

HARLEQUIN AMERICAN ROMANCE

1046—THE BABY'S BODYGUARD
1075—THE BABY SCHEME
1094—THE POLICE CHIEF'S LADY
1101—NINE-MONTH SURPRISE‡
1109—A FAMILY AT LAST‡
1118—DAD BY DEFAULT‡
1130—THE DOCTOR + FOUR‡
1149—THE DOCTOR'S LITTLE SECRET
1163—DADDY PROTECTOR
1177—TWIN SURPRISE
1209—THE FAMILY NEXT DOOR*
1223—BABY IN WAITING*
1242—MILLION-DOLLAR NANNY*
1273—DOCTOR DADDY
1295—THE WOULD-BE MOMMY**
1320—HIS HIRED BABY**
1335—THE HOLIDAY TRIPLETS**
1344—OFFICER DADDY**
1358—FALLING FOR THE NANNY **
1375—THE SURGEON'S SURPRISE TWINS**
1392—THE DETECTIVE'S ACCIDENTAL BABY**
1400—THE BABY DILEMMA**
1420—THE M.D.'S SECRET DAUGHTER**

‡Downhome Doctors
*Harmony Circle
**Safe Harbor Medical

Chapter One

Nurse Stacy Layne almost didn't hear the anesthesiologist's question. She disliked chitchat in the operating room, especially when she was assisting Dr. Cole Rattigan, head of the Safe Harbor Medical Center men's fertility program. His intense concentration and focused skill transformed microsurgery into an event more exciting than any Olympic competition.

Above the white mask, Cole's clear brown eyes fixed on the surgical microscope. Yet she got the sense he was seeing not only the incision but the whole patient, a man desperately hoping to reverse a vasectomy so he and his wife could have the children they longed for.

"Isn't today your birthday, Stacy?" anesthesiologist Rod Vintner repeated, while keeping one eye on the computer that monitored the patient's vital signs.

"Yes," she said tersely, staying alert for Dr. Rattigan's next move. It was her job, and her privilege, to provide him with whatever instrument he might require almost before he asked for it, so he didn't break concentration. To forestall further inquiries, she added, "I'm twenty-eight."

"Congratulations, Stacy," Dr. Rattigan said.

"Thanks." She beamed.

"Doing anything to celebrate?" Rod asked.

"I'll see," she returned noncommittally. Earlier, one of the nurses had invited a group to join him at a club tonight, but Stacy wasn't sure she felt like it. Her birthday didn't seem important, anyway, compared to the news she was anticipating. Possibly the most important news of her life.

"The egg bank should be sending flowers and chocolates." Amazingly, those words came from Cole Rattigan. Since joining the staff eight months earlier, the surgeon had maintained a pleasant but impersonal tone with her and, as far as she could tell, with everyone else. "I hear you're one of their first donors. How's that going?"

She gave a start, her hand nearly bumping the instrument tray. *He'd noticed?* Incredible.

"My couple…" She stopped to swallow, her throat suddenly dry. "The Barkers should be in Dr. Franco's office right now, waiting to find out if they're pregnant."

"Isn't that a first for the program?" Cole inquired.

"Yes. But we aren't sure yet."

Oh, please, please, please let Una be pregnant.

It was hard to explain Stacy's intense drive to bring babies into the world, even though they would belong to a couple she'd met only a few months ago. During Stacy's five years at Safe Harbor, she'd loved being part of the excitement as the hospital launched its programs for women's and men's fertility. At first, she'd expected that someday she'd be having her own babies here, but after her marriage shattered—*detonated* might be a better word—that hope had yielded to hardheaded reality.

It had taken time to get her bearings. Only late last

year had Stacy finally shed her married name, Raditch, for her maiden name, Layne. Then, at the beginning of this year, when the newly established egg bank began seeking donors, her purpose in life had fallen into place.

"Hold on." The surgeon peered through the microscope. "Too much scar tissue for a vasovasostomy. We'll just have to work a little harder."

Fortunately, the more complex alternative procedure, called a vasoepididymostomy, stood a good chance of succeeding in Dr. Rattigan's hands. As he revised his plans, his willpower filled the room with energy.

The rest of the operation flew by with little conversation. Stacy managed to avoid thinking about Una until the surgery was successfully concluded, sterile dressings applied, sponges, needles and instruments counted and disposed of, and her cap, mask and gown removed. Then, finally, she checked her phone's screen.

The text said: We're mommies!

Mommies.

Standing outside the surgical suite, Stacy felt blood rush to her head.

Too soon 2 no how many, the text continued. Several weeks ago, Una had been implanted with five of Stacy's eggs.

Yay! Stacy texted back, and tried to think of something to add. Maybe she should call. Yes, she ought to. Since the day she'd decided to donate eggs, Stacy had dreamed of this moment.

When she met Una and her husband—which was optional for donors as well as recipients—Stacy had felt an immediate bond with the heavyset woman. It had strengthened as they'd coordinated their cycles with hormones and underwent the egg retrieval and implantation procedures.

It was miraculous that Una had conceived on the first try.

I should call her.

The phone trembled in Stacy's hand.

Babies.

My babies. But they don't belong to me.

Abruptly, she felt as if her bones had gone hollow with longing, and her head began to spin.

"Are you all right?" A firm hand gripped her elbow. She caught the mingled scents of antiseptic soap and Cole's cologne, a blend of citrus and cedar. How embarrassing to have him see her this way.

"Just, um…" She managed to swallow, but no further words emerged. Her knees liquefying, she swayed toward Cole. When her cheek grazed his broad shoulder, she registered the smooth texture of his white coat, and felt his breath lightly ruffle her hair.

Stacy rocked onto her own feet. "Skipped lunch." A credible excuse, even though it wasn't true.

"You sure that's all it is?" His slightly shaggy eyebrows drew together in concern. "Might be flu going around."

"In May?"

His chuckle rumbled reassuringly. "Being from Minnesota, I'm still waiting for winter to hit. Seems like it's overdue. I'm sure I'll get used to Southern California's seasons eventually."

"I'd never risk exposing a patient if I felt ill," Stacy told him earnestly. "I'm fine."

That should have been his cue to stride off in his usual brisk, distracted manner. Instead, Cole stood regarding her with his head cocked and his brown hair rumpled from the recently removed surgical cap.

Impulsively, Stacy reached up and tweaked an errant tuft into place. Realizing how inappropriate that was, she drew her hand back. If he resented the impertinence, though, Cole gave no sign of it.

"I'd better make sure you get to the cafeteria safely." His mouth quirked. "Can't have my favorite scrub nurse falling and cracking her head."

She was his favorite surgical nurse? A velvety awareness tingled through Stacy. "I'm finished for the day."

"So I shouldn't care if you fall and crack your head?"

She ought to tease back, to prove that she'd recovered from her momentary weakness. Instead, she said, "Well, I do need a bite to eat. If you're headed to the cafeteria…"

"Cole! Got a minute?" The masculine demand wasn't really a request. Dr. Owen Tartikoff, chief of the fertility department and Cole's superior, had a way of appearing out of nowhere and startling everyone. Especially Stacy. If she found Dr. Rattigan a little intimidating, Dr. Tartikoff was downright terrifying. From his fiery hair to his piercing eyes, he seemed to threaten imminent career destruction to anyone who got in his way.

"I'm occupied," Cole responded calmly.

"I was just leaving." With a quivery smile, Stacy darted toward the elevators, leaving the men behind. The last thing she needed was to get caught in the crossfire between those two titans.

As the doors slid open, she wondered what her problem was. Not the flu; she didn't feel sick. Just off-kilter.

She ought to phone Una and invite her out for a nonalcoholic drink, Stacy mused as she headed toward the nurses' locker room. But that unexpected, unwanted, fierce longing to hold her babies in her own arms, to shelter and nurture them herself, had left her ill at ease.

She leaned against the locker room wall, missing Cole's support. Why did Dr. Tartikoff have to come barging in, interrupting their conversation and acting as if she were invisible? She ought to give him a piece of her mind.

The ridiculous notion of scolding Dr. Tartikoff restored Stacy's sense of humor as she changed into street clothes and collected her purse. Yet when she reached the ground floor, her footsteps carried her away from her usual route to the parking garage.

Instead, she followed a walkway that led to a set of bluffside steps. A late-afternoon stroll on the beach ought to clear her head.

The fact that she also avoided any chance of running into Una was merely a coincidence.

COLE KEPT A CLOSE WATCH on Stacy until the elevator doors closed behind her. Standing for hours in the operating room required serious stamina. If a surgeon felt his or her blood sugar dropping, he could call for an assistant to fetch a sandwich or coffee. Other personnel didn't have that option.

None of which explained his concern when he saw Stacy start to crumple in the hallway. Or the fact that he'd so enjoyed holding her steady.

He could still smell the perfume of her hair. It reminded him of a stroll through the daylily garden in Arneson Acres Park back in Minnesota.

"...decided to turn it into a lecture series," Owen

Tartikoff was intoning. "I've scheduled you for two weeks from tomorrow."

As Cole checked the calendar in his phone, his mind filled in the blanks in what Owen had said. Lecture—that was a clue. A couple of weeks ago Dr. T. had delivered an outreach talk entitled "Why Is There a Robot in My Operating Room?" To everyone's surprise, so many members of the public and press had showed up that the venue had to be switched from a small lecture hall to the hospital's main auditorium.

"What time?" he asked.

"Two o'clock."

Although Cole preferred presenting papers at medical conferences to addressing the public, he didn't object to speaking about his specialty. "I doubt that advances in men's fertility surgery will be a big draw, but…"

"We're calling it 'What's Killing Your Sperm?'" the fertility chief announced.

"That's an incendiary title."

"Exactly." A grin animated Owen's lean face. "Men's fertility rates are dropping. Hot stuff." He clapped Cole on the arm. "Glad you're free."

Steamrollered.

Usually Cole marched a step or two ahead of everyone around him. Not with Owen. Fortunately, Cole had nothing scheduled on the Saturday afternoon two weeks from tomorrow. If there'd been a conflict, he suspected he'd have had to cancel it.

He could refuse, of course. Owen's disapproval wouldn't bother him. However, now that he'd begun settling into his new position, a little publicity wouldn't hurt. He also hoped to become more involved in the hospital community. While schmoozing had never been his style, he didn't like to seem standoffish, either.

As Dr. T. swung off jauntily, Cole glanced at his watch. Nearly four o'clock. On the way to his office to deal with the usual accumulation of email, he decided to stop by the cafeteria and reassure himself that Stacy had arrived there in one piece.

He took the stairs down from the same-day surgery unit. During his first few weeks at Safe Harbor, sorting out the locations of various offices, operating suites, labs and other facilities had been quite a challenge. The odd layout, Cole had learned, was due to the way the hospital had been remodeled.

A few years earlier, plans to acquire a nearby dental office building and convert it into a high-tech fertility wing had fallen through. Rather than delay establishing its ambitious new programs, the corporation that owned Safe Harbor had stayed on schedule by converting facilities throughout the hospital, situating offices, labs and operating suites all over the six-story structure as well as the medical building next door.

Cole had found it awkward to have to ask directions from the nearest passing orderly or volunteer. Luckily, the practice of men's fertility rarely involved emergencies, so he'd taken the time to study the floor plans posted on each level. Now not only could he navigate, he often directed other staffers and visitors.

On the ground level, Cole followed the hallway to the gleaming cafeteria. The tantalizing scents of barbecue and spices greeted him from the hot-food station, evidence that the on-site chefs were preparing an early dinner. A fair number of nurses, orderlies and on-call doctors, including an obstetrician who worked a regular night shift, remained after most of the staff went home. No doubt they'd be trickling in soon prior to their evening assignments.

Cole scanned the expanse of nearly empty tables. No glimpse of Stacy's soft brown hair and full mouth. Perhaps she'd picked up her food and taken it to the patio.

At that moment, a compactly built man finished paying for a cup of coffee, and turned toward him. It was psychologist Laird Maclaine, a specialist in fertility-related counseling to whom Cole sometimes referred patients. When it came to emotional drama, he preferred to let an expert do the hand-holding.

Laird gave him a friendly nod. "Just the fellow I wanted to see. Any plans for tonight?"

"What's up?" He and Laird both cycled to work and arrived at the bike rack about the same time each morning. They often exchanged tips about bike paths and repair shops.

"The Suncrest Saloon's celebrating Elvis Presley night."

"Is it his birthday or something?" What a coincidence if the King of Rock 'n' Roll shared that date with Stacy. Casting a glance toward the patio doors, Cole realized he'd been thinking about asking her out for a drink. This might be a good excuse.

"Nope, that's January 8," Laird replied cheerfully. "Doesn't everybody know that? Anyway, they do this every few months. Music by the King and a twenty percent discount on Blue Hawaiians."

"What would I have to do?" Cole asked wryly. "Turn into a Smurf and bring a ukulele?"

Coffee sloshed and Laird had to sidestep to keep his shoes dry. "Don't make jokes when I'm holding a drink."

"Sorry. What's a Blue Hawaiian?"

Laird dropped a couple of paper napkins on the floor and pushed them around with his foot to sop up the spilled coffee. "It's a tropical drink. I have no idea what's in it but they're delicious. You interested?"

"Sure." Cole ought to get out more, so why not? As for the idea of inviting Stacy for a drink, he had no business putting his scrub nurse in such an awkward position.

"Really?" the psychologist said.

"If you didn't expect me to agree, why did you ask?" Come to think of it, Laird *had* extended a few previous invitations that Cole had declined.

The psychologist shrugged. "You may be the closest thing Safe Harbor has to a hermit, but underneath, you strike me as a regular guy."

"Thanks." Cole didn't intentionally keep to himself. However, he'd arrived in Safe Harbor last year still raw from a breakup with a smart, attractive and, as it turned out, aggressive attorney. Felicia's unsubtle hints about expecting a ring for Valentine's Day—with an implied *or else*—had triggered Cole's realization that he had no interest in marrying her. While he'd done them both a favor by breaking things off, she hadn't taken it that way. Her nasty insults on parting had stung, although they'd also confirmed the impression that she was the wrong woman for him. "Where is this saloon?"

"On Suncrest Avenue next to Waffle Haven. Right off the main bike path," Laird said.

"I do own a car." For safety, Cole normally drove after dark.

"You can't walk your car home if you overindulge." The psychologist moved aside to let a janitor clean up the spill.

"You can get a ticket for drinking and driving on a bike, can't you?" Cole recalled reading that somewhere.

"Maybe, but it's not likely unless you weave down the middle of Safe Harbor Boulevard."

"I'll take that into account." Cycling in the quiet of the evening amid the twinkle of house lights might be fun. "What time?"

"Nine-ish." With a wave of his free hand, Laird departed.

Cole decided against checking the patio. Most likely Stacy had left, and besides, she might mistake his professional concern for something more.

And I might mistake it, too.

Although he'd heard of several happy marriages among the Safe Harbor staff, workplace romances often backfired in an ugly fashion. And the person on the lower end of the power structure was usually the one who got hurt. Cole didn't intend to do that to Stacy.

He just needed to socialize more. Starting tonight.

Chapter Two

Stacy's walk on the beach carried her all the way to the harbor. Since she didn't feel like going home yet, she treated herself to a pita supper at the Sea Star Café by the pier. Seated outside, she relaxed in the salt air, watching sailboats glide to and from their moorings, listening to the slap of water and the indistinct voices of tourists sauntering along the wharf.

Her thoughts kept returning to her unplanned reaction to Una's good news. Once upon a time, Stacy had longed for her own babies, but only if she could raise them in a loving marriage such as her parents shared, and her sister had found. Sure, other women raised kids alone—including Stacy's roommate, a fellow nurse. But Harper, the widowed mother of a young girl, hadn't chosen to be a single mom.

Stacy wanted more for her biological kids. And she'd given it to them. A stay-at-home, Una had a wonderful husband, Jim, and an adopted two-year-old daughter. There'd be family support and full-time nurturing, like Stacy's mother had provided.

At twenty-eight, Stacy hadn't given up on happily-ever-after. But most programs required egg donors to be under thirty, so she'd felt some time pressure. As for her own future, she still didn't understand how the deeply caring relationship with her husband had fallen apart after only four years. True, the excitement and romance of their early days had naturally faded, but she'd considered that temporary, due to her busy schedule and Andrew's having to travel for an international investment company.

She'd believed she'd found the kind of enduring passion that had nourished her parents' marriage for more than three decades. But Andrew had fallen out of love, he'd said, and relit an old flame with his high school girlfriend, who was now his wife.

Surely there must be a man who could love Stacy with the same ardor her father felt for her mother, but since Andrew's betrayal, she found it hard to trust anyone. As for having kids, it might happen. Or it might not.

She felt a little ashamed of her reaction today, although she supposed she should have expected it. Her light-headedness might also stem from the arrival of her period. She'd seen a few signs this morning marking the end of her cycle.

She wished Dr. Rattigan hadn't witnessed her meltdown. He *had* been awfully sweet, though.

My favorite scrub nurse.

It might not sound like much of a compliment to anyone else, but it boosted her spirits.

Some of the nurses considered him a cold fish. In Stacy's opinion, *reserved* was a better word. Cole tended to observe people with a slight smile, as if he found them a fascinating alien species. So today, when he'd loosened up, it had been all the more special. She felt lucky to work with him.

As she walked back to the hospital, Stacy put in a call to Una. The mom-to-be was bubbling with high spirits. Judging by the happy noises in the background, she and Jim must be surrounded by family and friends. Stacy kept the conversation short and upbeat.

Afterward, she felt glad that she'd called, but let down, too. She'd expected to share in the joy when Una became pregnant, and instead she felt like an outsider.

She drove north to the apartment complex where she shared a two-bedroom unit with Harper and her six-year-old daughter, Mia. As Stacy mounted the outdoor steps, the mouthwatering aroma of baking drifted toward her, along with the chatter of children's voices through an open window.

"Quit dropping sprinkles on the floor!" That was Mia, a take-charge little personality.

"I missed my mouth, okay?" replied a boyish soprano.

"Stop eating all the cupcakes!"

"I only had two. Anyway, Aunt Stacy won't care."

That must be Reggie Cavill. Although not really Stacy's nephew, he might as well be. His late mom, Vicki, had been best friends with Stacy and Harper through high school, and they'd stayed by her side through her pregnancy and birth. Since her death in a car crash a few months ago, Reggie lived nearby with his real aunt, Dr. Adrienne Cavill, who also happened to be Stacy's ob-gyn. He often visited them and sometimes spent the night.

Glad to arrive home to a happy, noisy household, Stacy opened the door to a blast of yummy scents from the kitchen, to her right. Mia Anthony was perched at the table, her honey-brown hair falling around her face as she bent over a platter piled with cupcakes. Beside her, Reggie had managed to smear chocolate not only on the tip of his nose but also in his hair. As usual, he wore a solemn expression that made him seem older than five.

"Did I hear somebody mention my birthday?" Stacy teased, setting her purse aside.

"We did!" Reggie said artlessly.

"Are you ready for dessert?" Mia asked.

"Absolutely."

Stacy took scant notice of the toys and picture books littering the living room. It held a mishmash of furnishings, anyway, her delicate white sideboard and floral armchair nearly lost beside Harper's heavy, curved brown sofa and dark-wood entertainment center. As old friends, they'd made the best of things for the past few years, combining their meager budgets and housefuls of furniture.

Now that Harper had landed a better-paying job assisting Dr. Nora Franco, she could probably afford a larger place. Stacy hoped they wouldn't move anytime soon, although that might be more comfortable for Harper and Mia, who shared a bedroom.

"Since you like both flavors, we made vanilla cupcakes with chocolate icing," said Harper, drying her hands at the sink. An athletic five-foot-nine, she didn't seem the least tired after working all day and then picking up the kids at the hospital day care center. The woman was an inspiration.

"You are so thoughtful," Stacy said. "Thank you so much, all of you."

"Hold on." Harper plucked a box of twisty birthday candles from the counter. "Back off, kids. I'm gonna set these suckers on fire."

"Hurray!" Reggie hopped up, nearly overturning his chair.

Stacy rushed to steady it, and planted a kiss atop his

fuzzy head. He'd had a rough time, this little kid, with an absent father and an emotionally turbulent mom.

Harper began sticking candles into the cupcakes. "Somebody count."

"One, two, three!" shouted Mia.

"Four, five, six!" cried Reggie.

"That's enough," Harper said. "Right?"

"Plenty." Stacy didn't care about the candles. She was simply enjoying being there with her unconventional family. A duo of adorable handmade teddy bears watched the proceedings from a corner table. One wore a white coat and stethoscope, the other a pink nurse's uniform and cap.

They'd arrived yesterday from her mother and sister's boutique in Utah. Although Stacy had grown up in Orange County, her parents had moved to Salt Lake City to be near their elder daughter, her husband and their four children.

As the candles caught fire, the children stared with fascination at the tiny flames. "Don't forget to make a wish," Harper said. "I bet I can guess what it is."

"That one already came true." Stacy had leaned on Harper for support during her sojourn into the egg donor experience. "Una's expecting!"

"Wonderful." Harper nodded at the candles. "Well, wish for something else, and get a move on before the wax drips."

Closing her eyes, Stacy wished for…fun. She'd spent too much of her life worrying about other people, loving, losing, falling short, hoping and stressing out. It was time to enjoy being young, healthy and free.

Fun. Keeping that word in mind, she blew.

The candles winked out, drawing cheers from the children. Everybody grabbed a cupcake and began peeling away the paper. For the next few minutes silence reigned while they ate.

As she licked icing from her fingers, Stacy listened to Mia start in on a familiar theme: she wanted to adopt a kitten, like a couple of her school friends. The apartment complex didn't allow pets, however, so that was out of the question. It took all of Harper's persuasive abilities to draw her and Reggie into a discussion of which cartoon to watch before bedtime.

As much as Stacy loved spending time at home, watching kids' shows wasn't the kind of fun she'd wished for. She ought to check out that club, after all. She might even meet a guy. She refused to torture herself with fantasies about Mr. Right—just someone to make her feel desirable again.

From the moment Stacy had filled out the egg donor paperwork, she'd lost interest in dating. There had been too much else going on. Then, after taking fertility hormones this month, she'd been warned to avoid sex for the rest of her cycle. If the harvesting procedure had missed any microscopic eggs, the risk of a multiple pregnancy would be high.

Getting her period today would mark a fresh start. A re-birthday. When Stacy excused herself and went into her bedroom to change, she tucked a package of condoms into her purse. Not that she intended to go home with a man. Seeking reassurance after her divorce, she'd foolishly jumped into bed with someone she didn't care about, and suffered an emotional backlash afterward.

But playing it safe never hurt.

IT WAS A QUESTION Cole dreaded.

"What kind of doctor are you?" asked his dance

partner, a perky blonde woman. With the club brightened only by swirling lights, and echoing with Elvis Presley's baritone, there'd been little chance for conversation before they hit the floor.

"Men's doctor," he shouted over the music.

Her pretty features scrunched. "Come again?"

Why fight it? "Urologist."

The response was immediate. "Ick!"

It's not what you think. But how did he presume to know what she thought? So Cole merely shrugged.

The woman—he thought her name was Billie, but he might have misunderstood—gave him a look that said *Did you flunk out of every other possible specialty?*

"Thanks for the dance," Cole told her as soon as the song ended, and returned to the table he shared with Laird and Ned Norwalk from Dr. Tartikoff's office.

Laird had disappeared. Ned Norwalk, a tanned blond who went surfing most mornings before work, was slouched in his chair. "Not a keeper?"

"She didn't seem impressed by my specialty," Cole conceded.

"You should try telling her you're a male nurse."

He'd never considered Ned's occupation in that light. "I get 'ick.' What do you get?"

"They assume I'm gay." Ned shook his head. "Why do they think I'm here dancing with women if I'm not interested in them?"

"Surely you have plenty to choose from." In the cafeteria, Cole often saw him surrounded by female nurses. "You have a lot of attractive friends."

"My *friends* go and marry doctors," Ned responded cynically. "I'm surprised one of them hasn't snagged you yet. But you're new. Give 'em time."

Cole *had* intercepted a few interested glances, and

pretended not to notice. He'd always kept his work and his private life separate.

That made his sensitivity toward Stacy even more surprising. He simply liked her, that was all.

In a break between songs, Ned remarked, "Now, there's one I wouldn't mind getting to know better. Oh, damn. Laird beat me to her."

Before Cole could see who he meant, a waitress in a Hawaiian-print top and minuscule shorts blocked his view. "Refill?" She indicated the icy, blue-tinged glasses in front of them.

"What's in these?" Cole hadn't had a chance to ask earlier.

"Why do you care?" Ned asked. "They're great. Make mine a double."

The waitress nodded.

"I care what chemicals I… Just curious." Cole regarded the woman expectantly.

She rattled off the ingredients. "A Blue Hawaiian contains rum, pineapple juice, blue Curacao liqueur and crème de coconut, garnished with a cherry and a pineapple wedge."

One more couldn't hurt, he supposed. "I'll have a single."

She departed, unblocking Cole's view. Writhing bodies and spinning lights commandeered his field of vision. Among them, he spotted Laird's muscular shape gyrating close to his companion.

The scattered lighting coalesced into a soft glow, illuminating the woman. It picked out a hint of gold in her light brown hair and cast a rosy hue across her fair skin. Stacy must have recovered from her earlier shakiness. Still, dancing and drinking weren't what the doctor ordered.

Dancing and drinking with Laird were definitely not what *this* doctor would order.

The rapid beat of the music gave way to a slow rhythm. As the King's voice wove a seductive spell, Laird's hand claimed Stacy's waist and he eased closer. It seemed to Cole that she stiffened slightly before yielding.

"Wonder what she's doing here?" Ned mused. "She didn't seem interested in coming."

"You invited her?"

"Her and a few others. Guess it wasn't my lucky night." Cole's friend regarded him assessingly. "You could cut in."

"Why would I do that?"

"You can't take your eyes off her."

The waitress set drinks in front of them. After she moved away, Cole searched for the couple, who soon circled into view. Stacy winced as they got a little too close to another couple, and the other woman bumped her. Laird ought to pay more attention to his steering and less to the revealing V of Stacy's blouse.

"You think this calls for a rescue operation?" Ned must have noticed Stacy's predicament, too.

Tempting, but she'd probably come with a group of friends. Cole wasn't about to make a fool of himself by playing knight in shining armor to a damsel who'd brought her own backup.

He made a quick scan of the restaurant. In the dim interior, it was hard to pick out individuals. There must be several hundred people packing the dance floor and the ultramodern chairs and tables, their faces hazy beneath the spherical lighting fixtures. Above them, wall sculptures shaped like surfboards—or maybe they *were* surfboards—and tiki carvings loomed like fog-shrouded landmarks.

Laird had locked his arms around Stacy's waist. Rather than encircling his neck, she kept her arms in front of her protectively, bent at the elbows and nearly crushed between them. Why didn't the oaf respect her attempt to maintain a distance?

Irritated, Cole glanced at a straw lying on the table beside his slushy drink. The crushed ice might yield a pea-size pellet, he calculated, and he was a pretty damn good shot. Too bad he'd outgrown schoolboy pranks.

"You're right," he said. "She needs rescuing."

"Laird's full of himself," Ned agreed. "Go for it, Doc."

Cole rose to his feet and took a moment to adjust to the shifting light and the buzz of alcohol from his previous two drinks. Stronger than he'd realized, they were just hitting his circulatory system. Nothing he couldn't handle, though.

Getting his bearings, he carved a fairly steady course between the tables toward the dance floor.

Chapter Three

Stacy used to consider Laird Maclaine kind of cute. That impression was rapidly eroding. She didn't like being squeezed, and the fumes from the guy's breath were enough to make her tipsy.

Short of kicking him in the shins and giving him a hard shove, though, she didn't see how she could escape the rest of this slow dance. But if he tried to hang on for another, she vowed to take decisive action.

Coming to the Suncrest Saloon had seemed like a good idea. Ned was going to be here, and several other nurses had expressed interest in joining him. Then she'd spotted Cole at his table. While she'd debated whether to approach them, Laird had intercepted her.

The tipsy psychologist angled Stacy backward and down, dipping her in a show-offy move that nearly knocked her off her feet. How corny! It also pulled her blouse alarmingly low, revealing the lacy edges of her bra.

"That does it," she snapped when he hauled her upright, staggering a bit in the process. "We're done."

"We're just getting the hang of it," he said as the ballad segued into the more upbeat Elvis classic "Suspicious Minds." "We can't sit this one out."

"There is no we!" she shouted, and yanked free of his grasp.

She hadn't counted on him releasing her without warning. Propelled by her own momentum, she stumbled backward with nothing to grab on to, no way to stop her fall. Laird just stood there, gaping like an idiot.

For a suspended instant, the thought *This is a really stupid way to break my neck* blew through Stacy's mind. And then she collided with some hapless soul and they both went down in a tangle, while other dancers scurried out of the way.

She lay there stunned, trying to catch her breath. The man who had broken her fall was stretched beneath her. She could swear she felt his heart pounding through his shirt, although that might have been vibrations from the music.

"Are you all right?" Cautiously, Stacy sat up, straightening her blouse and feeling guilty as well as embarrassed. Even now, from this angle, she couldn't get a good look at the man she'd knocked to the ground.

To add to the humiliation, the deejay stopped the music. "Everyone okay out there?" he asked from his raised booth.

"I'm performing an internal diagnostic," responded a familiar voice from below Stacy.

She turned in alarm. Surely, she couldn't have collided with her own doctor. The surgeon she and the other O.R. staff protected against any potential harm to his hands or wrists, not to mention the rest of him. But there, unmistakably, lay Cole Rattigan, collapsed on the floor of a nightclub with his open-collared shirt askew and a puzzled expression furrowing his brow.

"Oh, my gosh!" Horrified, Stacy rose to her knees.

"I can't believe I bowled you over. Are your hands okay?"

He started to laugh, and then groaned. "Never mind the rest of me?"

"I meant… Oh, forget it. Somebody call an ambulance!"

Cole waved away the suggestion. "That would be overkill." Thankfully, he didn't seem upset that she'd created a spectacle in front of all these people, not to mention almost crushed him.

"Need help?" Laird reached down—to Cole, not to Stacy.

Cole regarded the outstretched hand as if it dripped with slime. "I suggest you assist the lady."

"Oh. Right."

Despite the fact that she had no desire to touch Laird ever again, Stacy let him pull her to her feet, while a bystander aided Cole. As they limped off the floor, the music resumed.

"No more dancing for me," Cole told Laird, who followed him. "I need to pay my tab."

"I'll get it." Laird clapped him on the shoulder. "Have a nice night," he said before wandering off.

"Moron," Stacy muttered.

"Don't let me spoil your birthday." Cole took a step and winced. "I think I might've sprained my knee."

"Oh, no!" Stacy took his arm, inhaling his scent. The antiseptic from earlier had been replaced by coconut. "You should stop by the hospital."

Cole hobbled beside her toward the exit. "Don't you know doctors never get checkups?" he said.

"Why? Because they're magically protected by the health fairy?" she quipped as they leaned their combined weight against the heavy door and spilled out into the night.

"Because we're royal pains in the neck who think we're God," he said grinning.

In the cool spring air, his body cast a heat shadow over Stacy. She resisted the temptation to snuggle closer to him. "Where did you park?"

He indicated a rack with two bicycles chained to it. "I think I'll call a cab."

"Don't be silly." Driving him home was the least she could do. "My car has a large trunk."

"I hate to put you out."

"No trouble." Stacy meant that. He couldn't live very far away, since he'd ridden his bike. "Stay here."

"Not going anywhere." Propped against the building, Cole halted her with a light touch on the arm. "I'm serious about not wrecking your celebration."

His hand remained there, connecting them. Stacy wished she'd been able to dance with him. A slow, intimate number.... *Stop it.*

"You aren't. And I can pick you up in the morning if you have surgery." He often scheduled operations on Saturdays.

"I wouldn't have gone drinking if I had." In the moonlight, his eyes held hers.

"Surely you didn't drink that much." To her, he seemed only a little more relaxed than usual.

"Two and a quarter drinks. I'm sure I'll metabolize them within a few hours," Cole agreed. "However, most people don't realize that your blood alcohol concentration continues to rise for a while after your initial intake."

"Initial intake, huh?" His formal phrasing, which

fit naturally into hospital conversations, rang oddly in the tavern parking lot. It was endearing.

"A moderate level of alcohol can be detected in your system for about eight hours. Sometimes longer," Cole continued earnestly. "I wouldn't take chances with my patients."

"You don't drink very often, do you?" she asked.

"Only on my favorite nurse's birthday."

"But you weren't with me," she pointed out.

"I can still celebrate the fact that you were born." His thumb traced her cheekbone.

It's not him talking. It's the alcohol.

Stacy drew away reluctantly. "I'll get my car."

Cole nodded, his coffee-colored eyes mysterious in the moonlight. "I await your return."

Someone had to take care of this guy, Stacy mused as she went to her vehicle. It might as well be her.

A sporty coupe and a boxy hybrid flanked her aged sedan. The semidarkness hid its chipped paint. Her parents had bought the car back when they had two daughters and their school friends to haul around.

Driving to the front of the tavern, she collected Cole and his bike, which he angled skillfully into the trunk.

Easing into the passenger seat, he flinched when he bent his knee. Guilt surged through Stacy. "That looks painful," she said from behind the wheel.

"I'll be able to stand just fine by Monday." He stretched out, taking advantage of the ample leg room.

"If not, I could hold you up while you operate." What had made her say that?

"That's an enticing prospect."

Following his directions, Stacy piloted them across the boulevard and along nearly deserted residential streets. Except for a few nightspots, Safe Harbor wasn't much of a party town. "What's Minneapolis like at night?"

"It's known for its performing arts," he responded. "The Guthrie Theater, dance, puppetry, a major arts festival."

"Do you have family there?" She had heard about a possible ex-girlfriend or fiancée through the hospital grapevine.

"Not anymore. My mother died two years ago."

"I'm sorry." Stacy couldn't imagine what she would do if she lost her mother. "You must miss her."

"I do. But we weren't especially close," he explained. "She was a general surgeon, worked long hours by choice. She loved operating on new body parts, parts she'd never removed, replaced or repaired before." He paused. "I shouldn't be talking like this."

"It's fine," Stacy told him. She understood his mother's fascination with surgery—and felt she understood him a little better, too. "Are you warm enough? I could turn on the heater."

"That's not necessary."

Or you could scoot a little closer.

She nearly smacked herself in the forehead for thinking that. From then on, she kept a firm grip on the wheel and her eyes on the road. Still, she could feel him watching her.

Stacy turned into the driveway of a modest ranch-style home. She was thinking it was a nice place for a bachelor, until he told her to pull up in front of a free-standing double garage topped by a small apartment.

"You live up there?" Stacy studied the staircase dubiously.

"It's cozy," he said.

"What about your knee?"

He followed her gaze. "There's a handrail."

If only I'd been more careful.

"Maybe your landlord will let you sleep on his couch," Stacy suggested.

"My land*lady* is notoriously nosy." Cole released an exasperated breath. "I suspect she's poked around my place once or twice while I wasn't home. If it wasn't so much trouble, I'd move. In the meantime, I'd rather not involve her."

Stacy would have offered up her couch, except that she lived on the second floor, too. And, come to think of it, Reggie was sleeping over tonight. "I'll help you," she offered.

"Good plan."

They tucked the bike into the garage through a side door. Glancing toward the house, Stacy saw a light on in what might be a bedroom, but no one came to check on them.

Together, they faced the challenge of the stairs, ascending in a series of steps and hops. Cole stood six inches taller than Stacy and had the tightly muscled build of a cyclist, which served him well as he balanced between her and the rail. Once, his knee nearly buckled and they swayed perilously. Stacy tightened her arm around his lean hips and firm butt.

Never mind that.

When they reached the top, they were both breathing hard. He keyed open the lock and they performed a dancelike maneuver to let the door swing out. "It's built wrong," Cole said. "It should open inward."

"That's odd," Stacy said as she slipped inside. She pictured her own door. Yep, it opened inward.

"My landlady had her brother-in-law install it on the cheap." Cole flicked on the weak overhead fixture. “I suspect they built the whole unit without the proper permits.”

The small living room, flanked by a kitchenette, must have come furnished. Stacy felt certain he hadn’t shipped the sagging, oversized sofa, dented coffee table and mismatched chairs cross-country.

The room also sported a big screen TV, a gaming system and a shiny laptop.

Guy toys.

Cole switched on a crystal table lamp and killed the overhead light. In the golden glow, the room transformed into a cozy lair.

“Better,” she said. “That’s a beautiful lamp.”

“I picked it up at a shop called A Memorable Décor. One of the employees there suggested it.” Cole limped to the refrigerator and peered inside. “I can offer you a range of reduced-sugar juices, which sound terribly boring even as I speak the words, or a late-night snack of cottage cheese, yogurt or leftover German potato salad that was tasty when I had it for dinner several nights ago.”

“Thanks, but I think I’ll pass.”

“Good. That gives me an excuse to suggest ice cream.” The small freezer section opened to reveal several tubs.

“Cole…”

“You’re right.” Without giving her time to finish, he closed the fridge. His mouth curving regretfully, he studied Stacy. “I can feel my alcohol level rising, and no doubt so is yours. Common sense dictates that you should leave. I just have one favor to ask.”

“Name it.”

“Wrap my knee before you go?”

"Of course." She should have thought of that. "Do you have a bag of frozen vegetables?"

He blinked. "I thought you weren't hungry."

"To use as an ice pack."

Cole grinned. "No, but I have ice. And plastic bags."

"I'll get one ready."

By the time she'd filled and sealed the bag, he was back, carrying a stretch bandage. He'd changed into short, blue striped pajamas. Under the circumstances, they seemed practical.

He lay on the couch, one knee raised atop a small cushion. As Stacy wrapped the bandage, being careful to maintain the tension, she appreciated his willingness to let her do her job. Whereas some doctors would have tried to direct every move, Cole simply observed her in silence.

What exactly was he observing?

Keenly aware of the quick rise and fall of his chest and of the way his eyes remained fixed on her, Stacy hoped her blouse wasn't gaping again.

"You have a light touch," he murmured.

"It comes with being a nurse," she replied.

"You're more considerate than most," Cole said. "I've noticed that about you. You can be sharp with Rod, not that he doesn't deserve it, and even a little prickly with me, but you're always kind to the patients."

"I'm prickly with you?" Stacy hadn't been aware of that.

"We all feel stressed at times."

The hormones she'd had to take as part of the egg donation process *had* affected her moods. "I don't ever want to take it out on my coworkers."

"You don't." He winced as she laid the plastic bag

over his bandaged knee. "That's cold." He shook his head. "Of course it's cold. It's ice."

Stacy chuckled. "You're a good patient. Most doctors hate being treated. They react like bears being poked with a sharp stick."

"We're a snarly lot." He shifted upward, propping himself against the cushions at the far end of the sofa. His hair was mussed again, Stacy noticed, and had to stop herself from smoothing it into place.

Instead, she rattled off the standard warnings about injuries. "Avoid anything that might increase the swelling. No hot showers, hot tubs or alcoholic beverages, as if I needed to remind you. And keep the knee elevated as much as possible."

"Maybe I'll sleep out here," he said.

"Good idea." She adjusted the cushion beneath his knee and lifted a comforter from the back of the sofa. "Did your mother crochet this?"

"My mother wielded a scalpel like an artist, but I doubt she had any idea what to do with a crochet hook," Cole said. "It was a gift from one of her nurses. Nurses often took pity on me as a child."

"They still do," Stacy pointed out as she draped the comforter over him.

"A familiar behavioral pattern—but different in this case." Without pausing to explain what he meant, he continued, "Would you care to watch a movie with me? I have a DVD in the player."

"I should be going." She was curious, though. "What movie is it?"

"Notting Hill."

She loved the romantic comedy with Hugh Grant and Julia Roberts. "It's one of my favorites."

"Mine, too."

"You're kidding." She wouldn't have pictured him enjoying anything so sentimental.

"The best romantic comedies provide real insight into male-female relationships," Cole said. "I also like action movies with crumbling temples and toppling statues of gods." He picked up the remote.

Her cue to leave…or stay. "We never ate our ice cream," Stacy said.

"And it's your birthday."

"Hang on."

Ice cream and Hugh Grant went together nicely. After they finished eating, unable to tear herself away, Stacy curled up beside Cole under the comforter. The movie was longer than she'd remembered, and she was getting sleepy.

Oh, well, where was the harm? she mused as she drifted off. She might be lying with her back pressed to Cole's chest, her bottom nestled against his groin and his arms around her, but nothing had happened.

Not yet, anyway.

Chapter Four

Cole awoke in the middle of an urgently thrilling dream. He was making love to Stacy, his body suffused with a delicious tension as he struggled to prolong the rapture of their contact.

As he blinked into awareness, he felt disoriented. A spring from the couch dug into his hip, while across the room a low crackling noise issued from the staticky TV. Most puzzlingly, his nose was buried in a tumble of lily-scented hair and his hardened member was pressed close against…

What was he doing?

In his sleep…in their sleep…Cole had almost had intercourse with his nurse. Now what? He doubted very much that this situation was addressed in any book of etiquette or medical code of conduct.

The longing was almost unbearable. Carefully, he tried to shift away from her without knocking her off the couch. "Stacy?" he said hoarsely.

"Oh, Lord, don't stop," she groaned, and ground her bottom against him.

That was all it took. In seconds, he'd done away with the thin fabric barriers between them and buried himself inside her. Her little cries of passion inspired wrenching moans from him, the likes of which he'd never uttered before. His need for her was primal and all-encompassing. Fire flashed through him, erasing everything but their astonishing fusion.

The flames faded, leaving him drenched in sweat. Holding Stacy, Cole gradually returned to a body he scarcely recognized. And to an ordinary room that had, briefly, become paradise.

He yearned for more—and knew he shouldn't have allowed this to happen in the first place.

She lay very still. "Stacy?" Cole whispered, almost afraid to break the silence.

"I can't believe we just did that." She tried to turn over, and nearly fell. Cole caught her and they balanced there, until she twisted around and swung her feet down for support. "This is..."

"Awkward?" He hoped he hadn't hurt her. "Are you all right?"

She coughed. "I'd better clean up."

Cool air replaced her heat. Cole pushed up to a sitting position until a sharp pain in his knee reminded him of his injury.

His head swam. Yes, there'd been a little alcohol involved. He couldn't blame that for his lapse in judgment, though.

In thirty-six years, Cole had committed his share of human errors. But never until now had he erred on so many levels. Yet he wasn't sure he regretted a mistake that had led to such a profound sense of connection.

Stacy returned with her hair tucked behind her ears, her skirt and blouse on straight and her skin glowing. She wasn't smiling, though. Or looking at him.

"Are you sure you're okay?" Cole said. "I hope this won't make you uncomfortable around me."

Sitting on a lumpy chair, Stacy clasped her hands in her lap. "I thought my period was starting, but I guess not."

"You can take a morning-after pill," he said.

She flinched. "I wouldn't feel right about that."

"Why not?" To him, it seemed an appropriate medical course of action.

"After all the effort it took for Una to get pregnant, I can't do that," she said, talking to a point on the wall. "I'd never even know whether..." She stopped.

Cole had obviously missed something. "Who's Una?"

Stacy blinked. "My recipient in the egg donor program. The program's first successful pregnancy."

"Then she *is* pregnant?"

"She texted me after surgery today," Stacy said. "It hasn't been announced."

He ventured to ask her something he'd been wondering since he learned of her involvement in the program. "Why did you decide to become a donor?"

She didn't seem to mind the question. "In December, one of my closest friends died in a car crash. Vicki struggled with alcohol addiction, and she lost the battle. It made me think about how I'd been in survival mode since my divorce, and that wasn't good enough. I wanted to do something lasting, something meaningful."

He would have reached for her hands had she been sitting closer. "And Una's the lucky mom."

"We went through a lot together. Now if I'm...well, I can't bring myself to take a morning-after pill."

That made sense. Still, Cole wasn't sure how to process the possibility of having a child. "Tell me what you need from me." They were in this together, although he wasn't sure exactly what that meant. His own mother had deliberately conceived him with a visiting art curator from France, who had played little part in Cole's life.

Stacy waved him off. "We only did it once, late in my cycle. How soon can I tell if I'm pregnant?"

"As a rule, a week to two weeks after conception." Cole often presented that answer to patients and their wives. "However..."

"However what?" Stacy appeared to hang on his words.

"Pregnancy tests measure the level of human chorionic gonadotropin, or hCG, in your body fluids. You know that, right?"

Her head bobbed.

"The hormone can only be detected after implantation, which occurs six to twelve days following fertilization." Noting the tension on Stacy's face, Cole hurried to the point. "However, since I'm sure you received an injection of hCG in preparation for harvesting eggs, that could produce a false positive. Let me find out more. I'm sure Dr. Tartikoff could answer—"

"No!" Her voice rose in horror.

An image of Owen's sharp features reacting to such a question troubled Cole, as well. "You're right. Not him. Maybe one of the other—"

"No." Stacy was on her feet now. "It'll be obvious soon enough. I mean, in a few weeks, right?"

"Certainly." Despite a throb in his knee, Cole rose also.

"Until then, let's keep this private." She rushed on. "If Rod gets the slightest inkling of what just happened he'll make our lives miserable."

Customarily, Cole paid little attention to the teasing—or more accurately, needling—that went on in the operating room. But Stacy's anxiety touched him. "If he bothers you, let me know. I'll make *his* life miserable."

She blinked. "I never saw this side of you before. It's almost…macho."

He felt ready to go into battle for her. "There's more where that came from."

Stacy started to laugh. "How sweet."

"Wrong adjective," Cole corrected. "Try *powerful. Manly.* Something along those lines."

"Okay." She grinned. "Don't punch him out. You might hurt your hands."

"I'll strangle him with his own tubing instead."

Stacy walked into Cole's arms and he held her close. An urge to protect her filled him, along with a resolve to keep their secret as long as she wished. Sharing it brought them closer.

"I'd better go." She backed away. "I don't want my roommate to start asking questions."

Trying not to limp, Cole escorted Stacy to the door. He'd rather she didn't drive home alone at night; it was nearly midnight, according to his watch. But in his present condition, he couldn't even walk her down the stairs. Thank goodness this was a safe town.

"I'll see you at work Monday." Stacy touched his cheek. "Have a good weekend, Doc."

He leaned forward and kissed her. The contact sent a surge of electricity through him, and then she drew back.

Cole wanted more. But he had to let her go. "Happy birthday. For the few minutes that are left."

"Thanks."

He watched as she descended the steps, and waited until her car pulled out of the driveway. Then he straightened the living room. He hesitated before shaking out the folds in the comforter, though. He didn't want to dispel the traces of Stacy's warmth.

What would they do if she was pregnant?

He supposed he'd find out soon enough.

IF STACY COULD HAVE SKIPPED the party for Una's pregnancy, she'd have gladly done so. She'd hoped the event would pass without any organized event, since both Dr. Tartikoff and the hospital administrator, Dr. Mark Rayburn, planned to keep the news from the press until the end of the first trimester. While everyone hoped for the best, the glare of publicity could only magnify the pain if Una suffered a miscarriage.

However, the small circle of staff aware of the achievement wanted a party, and Una herself seemed barely able to keep from spreading her happiness to the world. Stacy, having made no secret of her involvement, could hardly object.

And so, on the Friday two weeks after her escapade with Dr. Rattigan, Stacy finished her shift in the late afternoon, changed into a flowery spring dress and descended to the multipurpose room. Despite the pretense that this was merely a routine staff gathering, someone—she suspected the public relations director, Jennifer Martin—had draped the boxy room with bright pink and blue streamers, put on a recording of *Mozart for Babies* and stocked a buffet table with veggies, fruit, whole-wheat crackers and an array of cheeses.

Stacy slipped in, her attention focused on the food. Her stomach had been bothering her all day, and much as she'd longed to eat snacks, she couldn't do that during surgery.

She spotted Cole talking to the egg bank director,

Jan Garcia Sargent, and her husband of five months, Dr. Zack Sargent, who had performed Stacy and Una's egg extraction and implantation. Half-turned away from her, Cole hadn't seen her yet, and Stacy felt an irrational impulse to flee.

They'd continued to work together three or four times a week. The hardest part was assisting him with gowning and gloving before surgery. Pulling the sterile gown over his strong body aroused bittersweet memories. Easing the gloves over his large, square-tipped fingers reminded her of how incredible it felt when he touched her.

Each time, she'd covered up her reaction by maintaining a stream of idle chatter, double-checking special requests for supplies or equipment and asking questions she didn't really need answers to. She'd shut up only when she saw his attention drift away, no doubt to review the steps of the upcoming procedure.

After the operation, she always kept busy until she was sure he'd left the surgical suite. Then she hurried off to her next assignment or to the nurses' locker room via the most remote elevator. A few times when Cole had marched purposefully toward her, she'd either ducked down a hallway or started a conversation with someone nearby.

Cowardly, yes. But how could she tell him what she didn't know? As he'd pointed out, her hormone shots would render a pregnancy test inaccurate until enough time passed. Stacy hoped they also explained her churning stomach, light-headed moments and bloated sensation. Plus the fact that her period hadn't started yet.

She doubted it.

"There you are!" Una's cry seemed to echo off the walls as the mom-to-be fluttered toward her.

As usual, Una's multicolored outfit—a striped blouse and loosely woven pants—added to her larger-than-life impression. There was no avoiding the warm hug, or the way she stood there rocking back and forth with her arms around Stacy. Despite or perhaps because of growing up in foster homes, Una possessed a tremendous capacity for love.

Some of Stacy's edginess dissipated.

"I owe you so much," Una was saying. "You've made my dreams come true."

Stacy took a step back. "You look radiant."

"And big for my dates," Una responded cheerily. "I can't wait to find out how many I'm carrying!"

Her husband, a slender fellow with a receding hairline, swung toward them with their two-year-old daughter, Lynette, riding piggyback on his shoulders. She clapped her hands merrily. "Go, horsey!"

"Hi, sweetie." Stacy patted the little girl's hand.

"She's thrilled to be having a baby brother or sister." Jim jiggled in place to keep the tot entertained. "We didn't mean to tell her yet, but she overheard us talking. I'm not sure she fully understands."

That reminded Stacy of a matter she might soon be facing herself: how to explain an unplanned pregnancy to Mia and Reggie, to whom she ought to serve as a role model. All she'd wanted was to help others, to give something important to another family, and in doing so, to ease her sorrow at being unable to save Vicki from her demons. Now Stacy might be bringing a child into a less than ideal situation, with an unprepared mom and dad who were neither married nor likely to be.

Oh, please let me not be pregnant.

And yet, as Jan Sargent pulled Una and Jim away to accept congratulations from others, Stacy felt a surge of empathy. What if she and Una carried half siblings? Una wouldn't be the only one with a child in her arms....

Across the room, Cole caught her gaze and tipped his head toward a quiet corner. He wanted to talk.

Clearly, he took his role in the situation seriously. But Stacy had lost her heart once to a man who'd stopped loving her. She'd be very, very careful before she ran such a risk again.

Two weeks ago, with the thrill of their encounter still fresh, she'd tried to imagine Cole as a devoted husband like her father was. But despite the affection between them, their relationship lacked a romantic spark. No flowers, no tender text messages, no meaningful side-long glances. The Monday after their tryst, he'd seemed relieved when she focused strictly on how his knee was recovering, and on the surgery before them.

She should go talk to him. But first, her stomach demanded a commando raid on the buffet. Stacy pointed toward the food, and Cole conceded with a nod.

Her thoughts in a jumble as she crossed the room, she stopped abruptly to prevent a collision with the director of nursing, Betsy Raditch, who had the unfortunate distinction of being Stacy's ex-mother-in-law. "Sorry."

"No need to apologize." Betsy adjusted the half-glasses perched on her nose. It was hard to picture the unimposing woman as the mother of a brawny former college football star. "I was hoping to speak with you."

"About my schedule?" Scrub nurses were shifted around as needed, Stacy in particular, who assisted several surgeons and had no family obligations to limit her flexibility. Betsy could have made her life tough, but the nursing director had been fair despite the divorce.

"Is that the only thing we ever talk about?" Betsy sounded apologetic. "We used to have such interesting discussions."

"We did, didn't we?" During her marriage, Stacy had been thankful for their friendship. Later, she'd felt betrayed, realizing that Betsy must have been aware of her son's renewed relationship with his high school sweetheart before Andrew had informed Stacy of it. Perhaps Betsy also had a lingering fondness for Zora, who—to add insult to injury—worked as an ultrasound technician for some of the hospital's doctors.

"I admire what you've done for the Barkers," Betsy told her. "You always give so much of yourself."

"Thanks." She wasn't sure what to make of that remark.

"You look hungry."

"Famished."

"I'll let you go eat." As the older woman moved on, Stacy sneaked a look at Cole. Dr. Tartikoff had claimed his attention. She was safe, for the moment.

She hurried to get in line at the refreshment table. If those two tall women ahead of her would finish heaping their plates, she could finally eat.

One of them shifted position. It was, she realized, Harper, who noticed her at the same instant. "Stacy!" As if it were impossible to talk and serve oneself at the same time, she stood with a ladle of fruit salad in the air. "There you are!"

Nora Franco peered around her. "Congratulations!"

"Thanks, both of you."

Please keep moving.

"I'm so excited!" Harper said.

"Really? Why?"

Her roommate gestured at the throng of staff members surrounding Una. "Until now, your donation seemed kind of theoretical. It's finally sinking in that there's actually going to be a baby, or several."

"So there are."

Maybe more than you think.

Stacy took a deep breath to tame her protesting stomach. How long could her roommate stand with a ladle in midair?

"I'd like to be a donor."

Harper couldn't be thinking straight. "It's a rigorous procedure and you have Mia to take care of," she pointed out.

"I'm sure she'd understand." Her friend was getting wound up in her enthusiasm. Although sensible, Harper could also be impulsive. "I have no desire to remarry and I certainly don't want a second child on my own. But I dream about having a little boy, and it would be such a gift to give to a childless family. Well, I don't have to tell you! And then there's the money. I'd put it toward Mia's college savings."

"Five thousand dollars isn't that much, and you don't get it until they harvest the eggs." Stacy's stomach gave a lurch. It was about to embarrass her in public.

Setting down her empty plate, she made a dash for the exit. Thank goodness Dr. Tartikoff chose that moment to take the microphone and begin his welcome speech, drawing everyone's attention.

"This is a significant occasion for all of us...." His words boomed after her into the corridor.

From the corner of her eye she saw someone follow

her. Cole. He waited in the corridor as she flew into the ladies' room.

He'd implied that he meant to stand by her. That resolve, she feared, was about to be put to the test.

Chapter Five

Don't wreck this by overreacting.

In medical school, Cole had paid close attention to the Standardized Patient Encounter, in which medical students were taught to build rapport and show empathy while taking a medical history and performing a physical. He'd gained further experience in his practice, and usually established good relationships with his patients.

He wished there'd been a similar course in male-female relationships. Never having witnessed any interaction between his parents put him at a disadvantage. So, he was discovering, did a lack of romantic instincts, no matter how many Hugh Grant movies he watched.

For the past two weeks, he'd been reassured by Stacy's calmness. Working together felt comfortable. She didn't seem angry or emotionally fragile. He'd begun to think that her period must have started and she'd considered it too indelicate a matter to mention, although surely she knew better, given what they'd shared.

Then, a few minutes ago, she'd turned deathly pale and rushed from the party, clutching her stomach. Now, Cole struggled to maintain a composed air as he stood in the corridor outside the restrooms, just around the corner from the front lobby and information desk. Not that there were many people milling around, and not that he much cared what they thought. Still, as head of the men's fertility program, he owed the hospital a certain level of decorum. And he had to be careful to respect Stacy's feelings, whatever they might be.

It upset him to see her in such distress. If only he could find the right words to reassure her, and avoid any words that might hurt or alienate her.

The door to the ladies' room opened. Stacy appeared, looking very pretty in a flowered dress that reminded him of a watercolor painting. But worrisome smudges underscored her amber eyes.

Cole started forward. "Are you all right?"

"I threw up." She stared at him miserably.

"Does this mean you're…" He hesitated.

"I don't know."

This, at least, was a question he could answer. "Let's go to my office."

"Forget that!" she said. "You are *not* going to examine me."

"I just meant to give you a test." That statement didn't go over well. He could tell from the way she glowered at him.

"Let me handle this on my own." She pressed her lips together.

Cole took her hands. "I only want to help."

Her expression softened. "It felt like you were bossing me around."

"It did?"

Her short laugh ended in a sniffle. "Don't try to control me."

"I won't." He made a mental note to let her take the lead, even though he was the doctor.

"It's nice that you care about me." She moved closer, her hands small and warm in his.

"Of course I care," Cole said. "I'm the one who got you pregnant."

"What did you say?" The sharp-edged female's voice reminded him that they stood in full view of any passersby. He placed the speaker, a fair-haired woman in a no-nonsense suit, as Dr. Adrienne Cavill, an obstetrician who worked the overnight shift in the maternity ward and saw private patients a couple of evenings a week. Due to her schedule, their paths rarely crossed.

"Oh, Adrienne." Stacy slipped her hands free of Cole's and practically fell into Dr. Cavill's arms. "I think I'm pregnant."

"I warned you to be careful, this month especially." The female doctor took Stacy's arm. "We're going to my office right now."

"She's your patient?" Cole asked.

"And friend." Dr. Cavill cast him a piercing frown. "I take it you're the other half of this equation."

"It's not his fault," Stacy said.

"Fault?" Adrienne didn't wait for a response. "Let's not stand here debating."

"Agreed." Cole needed answers, and so did Stacy.

They walked together to the building next door, which housed medical office suites. Cole had joined a urology practice on the fourth floor. Dr. Cavill, he discovered, shared a second-floor suite with two other obstetricians, Dr. Rayburn and Dr. Sargent.

The waiting room was empty, as was the hall to the examining rooms. Cole was beginning to think they could contain this situation among the three of them when a short woman wearing thick glasses and a blue uniform peered from a break room. "Oh, Dr. Cavill. You're early."

"Finish your dinner, Eva," the obstetrician told the nurse. "I'll take care of Stacy."

"Hi." Eva gave Stacy a polite, puzzled smile. "Room three is prepped, Dr. Cavill. What supplies do you need?"

Stacy wrapped her arms around herself. Dr. Cavill paused as if unsure how to respond. Finally, she said, "A pregnancy kit."

Eva's gaze darted between Cole and Stacy, and a noise squeaked out of her. It might have been "Oh," or possibly "Huh?" Followed by, "Yes, Doctor."

Cole addressed the nurse in his best physician voice. "We can rely on your discretion, I trust."

"Certainly, Dr. Rattigan. I always respect patient confidentiality."

"I'll come with you," Stacy told Eva. To the other doctor she added, "I'll change in room three." The two nurses disappeared around a corner.

Dr. Cavill folded her arms. Although only of average height and most likely a few years younger than Cole, she had a commanding air that reminded him of his mother. Not the most welcome association, at the moment.

"So you're Stacy's friend as well as her doctor," he said.

The woman twisted an errant strand of hair into her bun. "She and my sister, Vicki, were close all through school, along with Harper Anthony."

Cole had no idea who Harper was, but felt as if he ought to.

"I see," he said lamely.

The obstetrician released what sounded to Cole like

an exasperated sigh. "It's not my place to lecture you on ethics, but I have to ask what the hell you thought you were doing with an egg donor who was still in her fertile cycle. Not to mention that she's your scrub nurse."

"I'm glad you decided not to lecture me," he returned mildly.

Some of the anger melted from her expression. "Point taken. It's just that I've watched Stacy claw her way back from a wrenching divorce to a man who didn't deserve her. She has the kindest heart in the world. Look at what she's done for the Barkers. She's generous and she's vulnerable."

"And you think I took advantage of her."

"Something like that."

Cole saw no reason to explain the odd circumstances under which he and Stacy had made love. "Would it help if I mentioned that my intentions are honorable?"

His colleague's mouth quirked as if fighting a smile. "That's an old-fashioned expression."

"Perhaps it should stage a comeback," Cole said.

Dr. Cavill glanced around the bend in the hall. Apparently the light over the examining room hadn't switched from red to green, because she returned her attention to him. "You're quite an enigma around here."

"In what sense?" he asked.

"We've heard how distinguished you are, how many papers you've published and how eager Dr. Tartikoff was to hire you," she said. "But you've maintained such a low profile, I had no idea you and Stacy were dating."

He decided not to disabuse her of that notion. "Some things are best kept private."

"This won't be private for long." She glanced at the examining room. "She's ready. Stay here."

He trailed after her. "This concerns me, too."

"I prefer to talk to my patient alone first. If she wants you in the room, I'll come get you." With a quelling look, the doctor whisked off.

Cole clenched his jaw and forced himself to stay put. Stacy had warned him against controlling behavior, and he meant to respect her wishes.

On the other hand, it was beginning to seep in that she might really be carrying a baby. *His* baby. Cole had never given much thought to that prospect, and wasn't sure how to react. Certainly not like a Neanderthal, crashing about and bludgeoning whoever got in his way.

But also not like his own father, who'd finished his term as guest curator at a Minneapolis art museum and flown back to Paris before his son was born. By making a pact with Cole's mother that required him to sire a child without further involvement, Cole's father hadn't considered how it would feel for his son to grow up with the painful awareness that his dad took no interest in him.

By middle school, Cole had insisted on his mother hiring a French tutor, and by high school he'd saved enough money for a flight to France. Jean-Paul Duval had greeted his son politely, escorted him about Paris as one might a guest, and talked at length about an exhibition of contemporary ceramics that he was curating. They'd spoken exclusively in English, and if he'd overheard Cole speaking with others in French, he hadn't remarked on it.

A week later, Cole had flown home with a chasm in his heart where warm memories of his father ought to be. He had, however, gained an appreciation for the inventive forms and ideas expressed by modern ceramic artists, and his tutor had remarked that his French was much improved.

Down the hall, the nurse was signaling. "You can go in now, Dr. Rattigan."

Cole tried to breathe normally, but he couldn't remember how he normally breathed. *"Merci,"* he said, and followed her.

"BECAUSE OF THE RISK of multiples, let's schedule an early ultrasound," Adrienne was saying when Cole entered. She paused, her brow creasing with the disapproval she usually reserved for Reggie when he performed gymnastics on the sofa or tried to hide broccoli in his pockets.

On the examining table, Stacy tugged the skimpy hospital gown into place. This was going to be a difficult pregnancy to manage, yet the possibility of twins or triplets made her decision to give up the babies easier, because there was no way she could raise multiples alone.

"I gather the test was positive." Cole gazed at her with concern. He didn't seem upset. Not elated, either, she observed sadly.

"Her hCG levels are nearly off the charts," Adrienne responded.

"An ultrasound's a good idea." Cole turned to Stacy. "How do you feel?"

Like the universe just caved in.

"Queasy." Not as bad as earlier, though, since Eva had provided her with a container of apple juice.

"I'll take you out for dinner," he said. "Or bring you some crackers, if you'd rather."

"No, thanks. I've got food at home and I'm kind of

tired." With her emotions in turmoil, Stacy preferred to be alone.

"I'd better go set up for the next patient." Giving her a sympathetic nod, Eva slipped out of the room.

That left Stacy with the two doctors, whose tense body language appeared to be directed at each other. She didn't like seeing her friends at odds.

"You can stop fretting," she told them. "I'll be placing it, or them, for adoption."

Cole gave a start. "Are you sure?"

"Don't pressure her!" Adrienne snapped.

"I wasn't," he replied sharply. "You should learn to distinguish compassion from control."

Great. They'd gone from glaring at each other to fighting. Stacy hated to think how the rest of the Safe Harbor staff—already overly invested in the belief that one person's business was everyone's business—might react to the situation.

"Listen, both of you," she ordered. "This is my decision, and I don't want the entire world weighing in. Let's be clear on that."

"*I'm* perfectly clear on it," Cole said. "However, this pregnancy is my responsibility, too."

"I'm aware that fathers have legal rights," she said, all the more irritable for her unwanted prickle of tears. "What are you planning to do? Sue for custody and raise a houseful of kids on your own?"

His mouth opened in astonishment. Finally, he said, "That's not even close to what I meant."

"Are you sure? I'd be happy to provide diapering lessons," Adrienne remarked drily.

"Very funny," Cole muttered.

Stacy ignored the exchange. If, in spite of her efforts, the doctors insisted on baiting each other, let them go at it. "There's no reason to broadcast my condition. It'll just cause embarrassment for the egg donor program, among other things."

Adrienne's eyes widened. "I hadn't considered that. Oh, my. What will Dr. Tartikoff say?"

"If he blows his top, I'll tell him to suck it up," Cole said.

Stacy laughed. It felt good to have him on her side when it came to the powers that be. "We're not telling anyone anything until I'm ready," she told Adrienne. "That includes Harper."

"I'll be sure to watch my tongue when I pick up Reggie tomorrow," her friend replied. The little boy was spending the night again. Although he stayed at a child care provider's home on the weeknights Adrienne worked, the sitter sometimes had family obligations on Fridays. "Eva will give you prenatal vitamins and schedule the ultrasound in a couple of weeks. That's the earliest we're likely to detect anything."

"Thanks, Adrienne."

When Cole helped Stacy down from the examining table, his touch felt cool and steady. "I'll wait for you outside," he said.

Stacy nodded. As soon as the pair had left, she began changing into her clothes.

Now that the reality of the pregnancy had begun to sink in, she wasn't as distressed as she might have expected. Giving life to more babies was a gift, not a tragedy.

Stacy recalled how, when she'd received Una's text saying We're mommies! a profound emptiness had swept over her. Another woman was carrying her baby. Now she had her own baby to carry.

And give to someone else.

Still, it was exciting to be part of the process, no matter how strongly her brain protested that she faced a long, uncomfortable road ahead. And that giving the baby up might be heart-wrenching.

Stacy's mom had told her once that she had a gift for reaching out to others. During high school, when her sister, Ellie, had gone through a rebellious phase, it was Stacy who'd brought her and their parents together to clear the air. When her mother went through menopause and became so grouchy she and Dad suffered a rough patch, Stacy had waged a campaign to remind them of how much they loved and needed each other. Now they were happier than ever.

She could endure a few tough months. The payoff would come when she saw how much this baby meant to an infertile couple.

Stacy emerged to find Cole leaning against the wall, his wistful expression brightening when he saw her. Suddenly, the next few months didn't look so bleak, after all.

From the waiting room came the murmur and rustle of patients. After making the necessary arrangements with Eva, she and Cole used a staff exit. Sneaking around like kids, Stacy thought.

Outside, the mild air reminded her that it was almost June. "I'm due in February," she blurted as they walked. "It's funny—I have to consider everything from a new perspective. Like Christmas…I'll be too big to fly to Utah."

Cole accompanied her into the parking structure. "Why would you fly to Utah?"

They knew so little about each other. "That's where my parents live now. They moved there to be with my sister and her family."

"Aha."

"Any more questions?" Stacy pressed the button for the garage elevator.

Cole cleared his throat. "Who's Harper?"

"My roommate."

When the elevator arrived, he got in with her.

"No bike today?" Stacy asked.

"Yes, but I'll see you to your car." The elevator gave a small lurch as it started. He put his arm around her waist and gripped the side bar with his free hand to steady them. "Did that hurt?"

She buried her face in his shoulder to smother a giggle. "I'm not that fragile."

"This roommate of yours, is she the helpful type?" Cole asked. "If you suffered a complication, would she know what to do?"

"She's an obstetrical nurse," Stacy assured him.

"Good choice," he said, as if she'd chosen her roommate specifically for that reason.

On the second floor, the elevator shuddered to a halt. Cole kept hold of her until they were safely on solid concrete.

They stopped by her car. As she dug in her purse for her keys, he said, "You don't have to deal with this situation alone. We should get married."

Stacy dropped her purse. Keys, Life Savers, tissues, a wallet and a phone spilled out. Thank goodness for the distraction, because it gave her time to gather her thoughts.

What on earth was she supposed to say to that?

Chapter Six

By the time Stacy had stuffed most of her possessions back into her purse, several facts had sorted themselves out in her brain.

She didn't want a marriage that was doomed from the start. She and Andrew had walked down the aisle madly in love, and look how that had turned out. How much less of a shot would a marriage have with a man motivated primarily by obligation?

She didn't harbor any illusions about a baby cementing the bond. Adorable as little ones might be, sleepless nights and crying jags took a toll. She'd seen how Harper and her late husband, Sean, had struggled to adjust after Mia's birth. Fortunately, a deep love for each other and a solid commitment had brought them close again before he died in an off-roading accident.

A baby deserved devoted parents, not a couple united by a drunken mistake. A real home, like the one Stacy had grown up in.

"I didn't put that very well." Cole handed her a lipstick tube he'd plucked from behind a tire. "If you'd like a more romantic proposal, I could arrange that."

As Stacy took the lipstick, her fingertips brushed his and the scent of his soap and aftershave teased her senses. She was tempted to smooth back his thick, brown hair, but that might give him the wrong impression.

"You're a good, kind man and a great surgeon." Despite feeling breathless, she pressed on. "But, don't think of this as our baby, Cole. In fact, it would be better if no one other than Adrienne and Eva knew you were the father."

"And let them believe…?" He stopped.

"That I had a one-night stand? So I did," she said. "Okay, if anyone—I'm not naming any names, but possibly Rod—makes any rude remarks, you have my permission to put them in their place. As my friend and colleague. Not as anything else."

He was watching her closely. "That's a no, then?"

"It is," she confirmed. "It's best for both our sakes. I have friends who'll be there for me."

"I'd like to be there for you, too," Cole said.

A temptation to give in to him nearly overrode Stacy's common sense, at the earnestness shining in his eyes. Then she remembered seeing that same resolve when a surgery turned difficult and Cole had to do everything in his power to save the patient.

This wasn't an operation he could wrap up in a few hours. This was their future they were talking about, theirs and the baby's.

"It's for the best."

She tried to ignore the disappointment in his face. The urge to please others might run strong in her blood, but she had to keep her priorities straight.

To forestall further discussion, she got behind the wheel of her car. Cole waited as she started the motor and backed out. In the rearview mirror, Stacy saw him still standing there as she drove off.

Somewhere, she reminded herself, there was a couple suffering for lack of a child. A couple whose empty arms she was going to fill.

That had to be enough.

SATURDAY MORNING, after surgery, Cole put together notes on the topic "What's Killing Your Sperm?" Although he disliked sensationalizing, perhaps the title would draw fifty or sixty people.

How fortunate that his listeners would never know the irony. In reality, Cole was annoyed with his sperm. Two and a quarter drinks ought to have sent the little swimmers to sleep for the night. Yet in defiance of all decorum, they'd had the nerve to impregnate Stacy. Yesterday, she'd practically collapsed at Una's party, and sitting on the examining table, she'd looked heartbreakingly vulnerable.

Why wouldn't she let him help? He almost resented those friends of hers. Without them, she might turn to him, which she should do anyway. This was his child, too.

Would it be a boy or girl? he wondered. Would it have his mother's nose or his father's eyes? Maybe it would be a little girl with Stacy's curly hair and elfin chin. If he saw her on the street someday, would he recognize her? And all this had started with one overachieving cell shaped like a tadpole and only a fraction the size of the period he'd just made in his notes.

Cole had two offices, one in the medical building, where he saw private patients, and the other designated for the head of the men's fertility program, in a ground-floor suite at the hospital. In his hospital office, he found a sports jacket on a peg and carried it to the doctors' lounge, which had a full-length mirror. Putting it on, Cole examined his reflection. Too casual? He replaced it with a white coat. Too pretentious? He felt ridiculous spending so much time deciding what to wear, yet he rarely appeared before the general public and wanted to make a good impression.

"I'd stick with the white coat." From across the lounge, Owen Tartikoff regarded Cole with amusement. Where had he come from? Whatever. On this occasion, Cole could use a second opinion.

"You think?" He frowned at his image. "I don't want to come across like some TV doctor."

"Image counts," the fertility chief observed. "But only if you get moving."

Cole checked the clock. Ten minutes to two. "Damn. I'm running late."

"Never thought I'd see you flustered about giving a little speech," Owen said.

Instead of dignifying that remark with a response, Cole asked, "Are you introducing me?"

"Got to babysit the twins." The surgeon rolled his shoulders. He'd been operating this morning, too. "Bailey has a rehearsal with the church choir. Don't worry. Jennifer Martin will warm them up for you."

"Does she know any male fertility jokes?" Cole asked.

"Those might play better at a urology conference."

"Good point." Cole returned to his office, rehung his sports jacket on its peg and hurried toward the auditorium. There were a lot of men milling around in the corridor, and a couple scowled at him when he angled between them. One large fellow made a move to block his path until he noticed the white coat.

"Are you the speaker?" the man asked.

"That's right." Cole indicated the congestion. "What's the holdup?"

"No seats."

No seats? The steeply tiered auditorium had permanently installed, well-upholstered chairs. He didn't see how anyone could have removed them.

A pretty, dark-haired woman peered anxiously from inside the double doors. "Cole!" It was Jennifer.

"Is something wrong with the chairs?" he asked as the man got out of his way.

"They're filled." She gestured for him to enter, and raised her voice to the men waiting in the hall. "If you don't mind sitting on the carpet, you can use the side aisles. For safety reasons, you have to leave space for at least one person to pass. Also, please avoid the area around the TV cameras."

The what?

"This way." The public relations director guided Cole down a side aisle, ahead of the sea of latecomers. How many people did this auditorium hold? he wondered, as heads turned to follow their progress.

Most of the crowd was male, with a sprinkling of women among them, Cole observed as he took a seat on the stage. As Jennifer had indicated, a camera crew occupied a post at the rear, which, given the steep slope of the room, put them at his eye level. A man with a couple of cameras dangling from his neck stood near the front, presumably also from the press. Who'd have thought the subject would attract so much attention?

When Jennifer reached the lectern, a profound stillness gripped the audience. No papers rustled. These weren't academics. They were people who cared.

"We are fortunate to have one of the nation's foremost urologists with us today," Jennifer began. "Dr.

Cole Rattigan is the innovator of surgical techniques that have become standard…"

His mind drifted as she summarized his education: University of Minnesota Medical School, Residency at Yale… The audience members leaned forward, listening intently. A few gripped tablet computers. Others held up cameras, presumably recording video. Everything he said was likely to be tweeted and blogged and posted online within seconds. How strange. That never happened at urology conferences.

"Without further ado, I give you Dr. Cole Rattigan," Jennifer finished.

Applause accompanied Cole to the microphone. Several microphones, in fact.

He got straight to the point. "Increasingly, or perhaps I should say decreasingly, we hear reports from around the globe that sperm counts are dropping to historic lows," he said. "How do we compare to our ancestors? That's debatable. It's not as if anyone ran around in ancient times testing sperm samples from the Visigoths."

Laughter rippled through the assembly. It felt good.

"However, there is evidence that during the past few decades, sperm counts have indeed decreased." He cited a few statistics. "It isn't only the number of sperm that affect fertility. There's also motility—the ability to swim—along with speed, concentration and morphology, which means shape and size."

The only noise came from fingers tapping on laptop keys and the scratch of pens on paper. Cole hadn't said anything interesting yet, just provided some basic background.

"What's causing this?" he asked rhetorically. At the back of the auditorium, a few more latecomers slipped in and stood against the wall.

"The easy answer is to blame the environment." Cole didn't bother reading his notes. Everyone knew this stuff—well, everyone in his field. "Toxins in our food, our air and our water. But it isn't that simple. Our genetic programming and our social mores have an impact, too."

He explained that since sperm-producing genes exist only on the Y, or male, chromosome, there was no way for the body to compensate for a degraded gene with a healthy one from the X chromosome. In time, this situation could cause birth rates to dwindle. Most species compensated with promiscuity.

"It may not seem very nice," he said, "but the result is that the guy with the healthiest sperm sires a lot of children, while the guy with weak sperm doesn't reproduce. That might sound like we'd lose a lot of Einsteins and gain a lot of action heroes, but we shouldn't equate rough-and-ready sperm with rough-and-ready physiques."

A few chuckles greeted this remark. Well, Cole had never claimed to be a stand-up comic.

"Sad to say, the use of anabolic steroids to increase muscle mass and improve athletic ability is widespread. These steroids may be male hormones, but ironically, they suppress a man's ability to manufacture testosterone. Some of the side effects can persist across one's lifetime," he added.

"Our personal medical histories and lifestyles also affect fertility." Among the harmful factors, Cole listed infections, smoking, obesity, poor diet, too much or too little exercise, illegal drugs, and both prescription and over-the-counter medications.

Okay, he'd scared them enough. "On the plus side, many of the conditions killing or impeding sperm can be fixed. Sometimes weight loss, improved diet, vitamin supplements and a healthier lifestyle will do the trick. Other times, surgery or advanced fertility techniques can help a man to father children."

He described some of the newer treatments, and concluded, "There's research under way that may allow even men with no sperm to become fathers by using their stem cells. So far, it's only been tested on mice, but then, it's a mere thirty-five years since the first test tube baby was born, and more than four million infants have been born in vitro since then. Yesterday's miracle is today's standard course of treatment."

Cole expected the usual smattering of applause. Instead, a swell swept through the auditorium as the listeners rose to their feet. What had he said? He'd just reiterated facts known by everyone in his profession.

Finally, the ovation ebbed and people sat down. "Any questions?" Cole asked.

Hands flew up. He pointed to a husky fellow in the center.

"This was interesting, but when a couple can't have a baby, isn't that mainly the wife's problem?"

A woman in the audience hissed. Cole figured she'd like his response. "Quite the opposite. In about sixty percent of infertility cases, the man's condition is involved. Twenty percent involve both the man and the woman, and forty percent are mostly him. Since running a sperm analysis is relatively simple, that should be one of the first tests to consider."

More hands went up. Before Cole could choose from among them, a tall man with abundant wavy hair shouted from near the cameras, "So are you saying there's a danger of the human race fading away?"

Normally, Cole would have laughed off such a ridiculous question, but he knew enough not to dismiss the press. "Well, if we relied on technology to reproduce for a few millennia, and then an asteroid knocked us back to the Stone Age without modern medicine, we could be in trouble." He had to smile at such an unlikely scenario. "But—"

"So you're saying we may be evolving into a species unable to survive without doctors?" interrupted a heavily made-up woman in a power suit.

Cole decided to provide a bit of perspective. "In a similar vein, one could argue that vaccines and antibiotics interfere with our developing genetic immunities. Should we let millions of people die from treatable or preventable diseases, and let the survivors and a few naturally immune individuals repopulate the planet?"

Jennifer scooted to the microphone, which Cole gladly relinquished. "I see we have a lot of questions." Deftly, she began calling on ordinary folks who wanted to know about testing, surgery and outcomes.

Fifteen minutes later, although there were still hands waving, Jennifer apologetically ended the session. "I'm afraid we can't get to everyone. If you'll email your questions to the public relations office, I'll forward them to Dr. Rattigan. Thank you all for coming."

"I wouldn't mind answering their questions," Cole told her as she led him off the stage. "I'm in no hurry."

"We have security personnel whose shifts are ending," she explained. "And I promised Ian I'd relieve him of babysitting duties so he can conduct an interview."

Cole recalled that her husband, a journalist and author, hosted an online news focus show.

"I see," Cole said. "Thanks for your help."

"I didn't expect this big a turnout," she admitted. "You handled the press well."

"They tend to ask silly questions." He had received his share of accolades and awards over the years, but he'd never before had an experience like this with the media.

"They aren't all so superficial," Jennifer said as they skirted the remnants of the crowd. "Ian explores serious issues on his show. Still, he couldn't earn a living doing that. Serious journalism rarely goes viral."

Cole held a side door for her. "I don't understand why anyone would want to be famous," he said, right before he stepped out into the glare of camera flashes.

Chapter Seven

With microphones in his face and questions flying, Cole did his best to answer the barrage of increasingly ridiculous questions. Should schools teach teenage boys to preserve the health of their sperm? Should the federal government create an office to combat the decline in male fertility? Should there be a law against tight-fitting men's underpants, since these could raise the temperature enough to damage sperm?

His struggles to keep a straight face soon gave way to frustration. A handful of men were waiting to one side, clearly eager to ask about their personal situations, while the reporters ignored Jennifer's attempts to wrap up the impromptu press conference. A security guard hovered, held in check by the PR director's warning frown. You didn't manhandle the press.

All the same, Cole feared that if this went on much longer, he might lose his temper and become sarcastic. His tongue had sliced and diced more than a few bullies in his early years, but those individuals hadn't had the power to edit his comments and make him look like a bad-tempered idiot on the air.

"As a fertility doctor, aren't you adding to the crisis

of unwanted babies?" demanded a man whose T-shirt bore the call letters of a Los Angeles radio station.

Cole hardly knew where to start. "Men who undergo treatment aren't likely to abandon their children. And if there's a crisis of unwanted babies, why are so many couples adopting overseas?"

"Isn't the whole infertility field just a racket to make doctors rich?" the reporter persisted.

Cole found himself at a rare loss for words. Mercifully, a series of loud claps cut off the other reporters' attempts to leap into the breach.

From among the men waiting at the side, a blond fellow built like a wrestler stalked in front of the reporters. "You folks have had your turn," he boomed. "Now mind your manners and give the rest of us a chance."

"Who are you?" someone demanded.

"I'm a high school biology teacher used to setting boundaries for adolescents." The statement drew muffled laughter.

"The public has a right to know," a female journalist snapped.

"Yeah, you're not in charge here," a radio reporter interjected.

"Ever heard of showing respect for others?" the teacher responded. "If you were my students, I'd send you all to the principal's office."

Seizing his chance, the security guard moved in. "Folks, fire regulations require me to clear the corridor. If you'll just head toward the exits…"

"Thank you for coming," Jennifer called, and grabbed Cole's elbow. "Quick! Hide!"

Most of the waiting men scattered, along with the press. Spurred by a sense of fair play, Cole waved to the teacher to come with them.

They ducked into the fertility program suite. It being a Saturday, there was no one else around.

"Thanks, Jennifer," Cole told the PR director as he unlocked his private office. "You've been great."

"You sure you're all right?" She seemed uncertain about their guest.

"Go home to your family." Speaking those words gave Cole a twinge. Until recently, families had belonged to other people, not to him. Now his thoughts flew to Stacy and the baby she carried.

She'd told him to mind his own business. Yet wasn't it his business, too?

To the teacher, Jennifer said, "I'm Jennifer Martin, by the way, and you did a great job of running interference."

"Peter Gladstone. My motives were purely self-serving." They shook hands. After she departed, he accepted a seat. "I appreciate your sparing me a few minutes, Dr. Rattigan."

Behind his desk, Cole shifted into doctor mode. "What can I do for you?"

"I'm trying to find out if there's any point in my even making an appointment. My case might be hopeless."

"What seems to be the problem?" Normally, Cole would have insisted they continue this discussion during an office visit, since he couldn't assess the situation without a medical history or an examination. However, in view of Peter's help earlier, he felt the guy deserved more than a quick dismissal.

The man folded his muscular arms. "I have a low sperm count. My previous doctor ruled out a number of factors, but he couldn't find a cause."

Mentally, Cole struck off the man's age—early thirties—and apparently good health as possible causes. “He didn’t give you a referral?”

“He never got the chance. My wife...” The teacher’s voice broke.

Cole refrained from offering sympathy. In his experience, guys who got emotional preferred to pretend you hadn’t noticed.

Peter swallowed and went on. “During the fertility workup, we discovered my wife had ovarian cancer. She died a year and a half ago.”

“I’m sorry.” He was confused. “Why are you concerned about your sperm count now?”

“Having children has always been my dream,” the teacher said. “I can’t believe I’ll ever find anyone I could love as much as Angela, but even if I do, how could I ask her to marry me if I can’t father children?”

He could find someone who loved him enough to adopt or to use artificial insemination, but this wasn’t a counseling session, and Peter was smart enough to have considered those ideas on his own. Obviously, he wanted his own flesh-and-blood children. “Do you remember what tests have been run?”

Peter’s expression cleared at the straightforward question. “Yes, I do.” He read off a list of tests and results from his cell phone. The previous physician, a local urologist, had done a thorough job.

Although they’d exhausted the obvious possibilities, that wasn’t the end of the story. “I’d like to review your case in more depth,” Cole told Peter. “If you have any trouble getting an appointment, ask for my nurse, Luke Mendez.” Cole typed on the computer as he spoke. “I’m sending him an email right now. We’ll schedule you in.”

Gratitude suffused the man’s face. “I can’t tell you how much this means to me.”

"I'm glad to help."

After his visitor left, Cole made a few notes while the discussion was fresh in his mind. Peter's determination to have children underscored the irony of Cole's own impending fatherhood.

What was he going to do about it? The prospect of standing aside, preserving his anonymity and watching Stacy take the heat as she grew ever larger struck him as unacceptable. And what about their baby?

Working in a hospital, he saw babies all the time. Their presence barely registered, though. Taking a closer look might help guide his reaction.

After locking his office, Cole climbed to the third floor. While most of the hospital lay quiet on a Saturday afternoon, there was plenty of activity around Labor and Delivery. During his internship, that hadn't been one of his favorite rotations. Too much noise, too many hard-to-control factors and too many relatives swamping the waiting rooms and demanding updates.

Also, Cole had been so absorbed in the medical details of delivering babies and attending to the mothers that he'd paid little attention to the infants. Yes, there'd been a rush of appreciation every time he held a newborn, but he'd also been sharply aware of their fragility, and was happy to transfer them into someone else's capable hands. Once they were safely delivered, they belonged to the nurses, pediatricians and, of course, the parents.

He followed the signs to the viewing window at the nursery. Prepared for a vista of tiny people, Cole stared in dismay at the mostly empty bassinets. Only a few little ones lay sleeping beneath the attentive eye of a nurse, and they weren't close enough to the window for him to see well.

A passing doctor, dark-haired with a short mustache, paused to ask, "What brings you here, Cole?" His name tag read Jared Sellers, M.D., Neonatologist.

Cole had no intention of explaining his reasons, especially to someone he only vaguely recognized. Still, he appreciated the other doctor's courtesy. "Are all the babies in the patients' rooms?"

Jared nodded. "You'll see more of them in intermediate care, just around the corner."

"Thanks."

"Not too many urologists drop by to visit the babies."

Was the staff always this curious? "Maybe they should." Impulsively, Cole added, "Do you have kids?"

Out came the cell phone, and an image of a baby appeared, a pink bow decorating her reddish-brown curls. "That's my daughter, Bonnie. She's two months old," the neonatologist said. "My wife, Lori, is on leave from her job as Dr. Rayburn's nurse. I'm not sure if she can bear to go back to work in another month and put our little girl in day care."

This was more information than Cole wanted. "She's adorable." That seemed like the right thing to say.

"And supersmart," Jared enthused. "She's curious about everything. For her age, she has great head and neck control."

Cole had never considered babies interesting until they achieved such milestones as sitting up, standing or talking. Obviously, parents noted small markers that he'd never considered.

Will I be like that?

What was he thinking? He wasn't going to be around. No photos in his cell phone. No idea how his son or daughter was developing.

He'd better get moving before the other doctor repeated the question about what he was doing there. "I'd better be off," he said. "Congratulations on your daughter."

"Thanks." Jared was too busy reviewing images—quite a few, apparently—to glance up from his phone.

Cole debated stopping by the intermediate care facility, but his initial impulse to view babies now seemed ill-considered. Instead, he went outside to his bike. He'd resumed cycling to work once his knee recovered, and he was glad now for the exercise. It helped settle his thoughts.

As he pumped along Hospital Way, one theme emerged. He had to talk to Stacy about how they were going to manage this pregnancy. That was his baby in there, and while he respected her right to give it up for adoption, he intended to be involved until it was delivered.

STACY STAYED IN BED most of Saturday morning, sipping orange-flavored herbal tea. Her troublesome stomach had gone into overdrive, leaving her perpetually queasy and sleepy.

If only her mother were here to fix toast and fuss over her. Several times, Stacy reached for the phone to call her, but she didn't feel up to explaining everything. Besides, Ellen Layne led a busy life, running a shop, making stuffed animals and helping her namesake, Stacy's older sister Ellie, care for her four children.

Then there was Dad's reaction to consider. Alastair Layne had always been meticulous both in his work as a pharmacist and in raising his daughters. Other girls were allowed to wear skimpy clothing and have multiple piercings, but not Stacy or Ellie. After learning about Andrew's infidelity, he'd backed Stacy in the divorce, but had remained noncommittal on the subject of egg donation, apparently unsure where that fit into his moral continuum.

Out-of-marriage pregnancy was unquestionably on the low end. He'd be terribly disappointed in her. Stacy had no idea how he'd feel about her giving up the baby for adoption versus keeping it, and she wasn't eager to find out.

Maybe she could avoid telling them altogether. That would require avoiding them for the next eight months and lying about it, though. She decided against dealing with the issue while she felt lousy.

After a light lunch, she dragged herself to the supermarket, then came home and put the food away. A note from Harper indicated she'd taken Mia to a birthday party for her friend Fiona, the daughter of the hospital's embryologist.

After surfing the internet for a bit, Stacy lay down on the couch. She hoped her roommate would come back soon so they could talk. This pregnancy was going to affect Harper, so she had a right to hear about it from Stacy before word got out, or Harper picked up early signs of pregnancy on her own.

Stacy must have drifted off, because a ringing sound dragged her from the depths. Disoriented, she groped for her phone. How long had she slept?

Two hours, according to her watch. It was nearly 5:00 p.m. Harper must have stayed at the party, which, Stacy recalled from the invitation posted on the refrigerator, ran from 4:00 to 7:00 p.m.

"Stacy?" It was Cole.

"Is something wrong?" she asked sleepily.

"Wrong?"

"Am I late for surgery?" No, wait, it was Saturday.

Besides, if she were late for work, a supervisor would be calling, not the doctor. “What’s up?”

“I thought I’d bring dinner.” Determination underscored his words. “I’m partial to pesto ravioli from Papa Giovanni’s but, if you’re craving something else, just say so.”

She should refuse, but her stomach was crying out for food, and she missed Cole. That melting expression, that special smile… Harper wouldn’t be back for another hour and a half, so they could enjoy some privacy. “I’d love that.” She gave him her address.

“Great!” he exclaimed, as if she’d done him a huge favor. “See you in a few minutes.”

Stacy noted the toys and papers scattered around the room. What a contrast to Cole’s scrupulously neat place. As if to compensate for the day’s languor, a surge of energy sent her flying around the apartment to put away the mess.

Then she caught a frightening glimpse of herself in a mirror, hair bristling like a porcupine’s, eyebrows askew, lips pale. She charged into the bedroom to fix her hair and makeup.

She was almost ready when she heard the scrape of a key in the front door. Her roommate was back early. How was Stacy going to explain Cole’s visit?

With the truth, she supposed.

Willing herself to be calm, she strolled into the front room. Harper had dumped a sheaf of papers on top of the coffee table, which Stacy had cleared only minutes earlier. The dark-haired nurse regarded her with excitement and a touch of apprehension.

There was no sign of Mia, who must still be at the party. “What’s all this?” Stacy asked.

"You're going to kill me." Her friend clasped her hands together. "Don't be mad, okay?"

"Why would I be mad?"

"Well, you know how Mia's been longing for a kitten," Harper began.

"You got a kitten?" Stacy glanced around. No furry little animal. No bags of cat food or kitty litter, either. "That would violate our lease."

"Yes. So?" She didn't understand why her normally forthright roommate was beating around the bush.

"Last night at the reception for Una—where did you go, anyway?"

"Never mind." Stacy refused to be distracted. "Talk."

Harper waved her hands. "I told you I'm planning to donate eggs, right?"

"You said you were considering it."

"It didn't seem fair to Mia to get involved in something so complicated and stressful," Harper went on. "Especially when I won't even let her have a pet."

Stacy sat on the couch. "I don't see how the two things are related."

"Give me a minute to connect the dots." Harper fingered her hoop earring. "At the party, I was talking to Caroline Carter—you know, the fertility department secretary—and she mentioned a house for rent in her neighborhood. They allow pets. It's been off the market because of some major plumbing work. Once they start advertising, it'll get snapped up fast."

Dismay swept over Stacy. The papers on the coffee table must be a lease. "You're moving?"

How could she bring a stranger into this situation? Still, it wasn't Harper's job to serve as her caretaker.

"I know this is sudden." Her roommate studied her worriedly. "But we always said this was a temporary arrangement. I'm earning more now that I'm working for Dr. Franco. I guess the whole business with Una made me realize how I've put my life on hold since Sean died. My life and Mia's, too. This house becoming available seems like, well, like a sign."

Stacy didn't want to put a guilt trip on her friend. Harper had no idea about her pregnancy, and Stacy decided not to lay that on her right now. "When?"

"Next weekend," Harper said apologetically.

"That soon?" How was she going to find a roommate by then?

Her friend produced a sheet of paper. "I made a list of hospital personnel who might want to share an apartment. Think of the advantages. No more kid stuff everywhere, and you can bring the rest of your furniture out of storage."

Stacy *did* miss the sofa and end tables that hadn't fit in the living room, plus she'd save money not having to pay for storage. But that was a small consolation.

I was counting on you.

Gazing into the apologetic face of the woman who'd been one of her best friends since middle school, Stacy bit back the words. The two of them had shared grief over Sean's and Vicki's deaths and the demise of Stacy's marriage. The rotten timing wasn't Harper's fault.

"I'll throw you and Mia a housewarming party once you've settled in." Stacy glanced at the list of potential roommates. "Meanwhile, I'll start calling some of these people."

"I'll help. Thanks for understanding, Stace."

"Of course I do."

The bell buzzed. Harper started for the door. "Who do you suppose that is?"

In the shock of her roommate's news, Stacy had almost forgotten about Cole's visit. "Wait! I'll get that," she said.

Too late. The door was already open, and the pair of them were face-to-face. Unless Stacy intervened, they were likely to tell each other things she wasn't ready for them to share.

Chapter Eight

"Dr. Rattigan?" Harper sounded confused.

"Is...? Oh, there she is." Cole's expression warmed. As she approached the door, Stacy caught the enticing scents of basil and garlic from the sacks he carried.

She yearned to hug him and snatch the food from his hands.

Must be my crazy, mixed-up hormones.

"Hi, Cole," she managed to say. "This is Harper."

Still in the doorway, he returned his gaze to her roommate. "I've seen you at the hospital, haven't I?"

"Yes. What are you...?" Perhaps realizing that she had no business cross-examining Stacy's guest, Harper backed off. "Come in."

This was growing more awkward by the moment. "Don't you have to go pick up Mia?" Stacy asked.

"Not for fifteen minutes."

"Well, don't you have to go *somewhere?*" If Harper found out about the pregnancy, she'd be racked by guilt about leaving. And if Cole learned that Stacy was being left alone...

He'd do what? Renew his offer of a marriage of convenience? Seriously, nobody did that sort of thing.

Or he might suggest moving in.

The scary part was, she kind of liked the idea. Having him around felt safe and comforting. And sexy, too, now that her earlier queasiness had subsided.

The two of them, living together as she ballooned with his baby? So much for keeping his paternity secret. Stacy cringed at the prospect of them becoming the butt of everyone's jokes. More important, they weren't in love. No matter how impractical her attitude might seem to others, Stacy meant to hold out for the real thing, an all-encompassing, everlasting love like her parents shared.

"You brought supper?" Harper was asking. "That smells wonderful. Are you two, uh, dating? Not that I'm trying to be nosy, but Stacy didn't mention it."

This conversation felt like a runaway train. Stacy's mind scrabbled frantically, trying to figure out how to throw the switch. "He's only being, uh…"

"Supportive, although I'm glad she has such a close friend to help her through her pregnancy," Cole said.

Crash. Train derailed. Or, more accurately, smashing right through the station, littering the ground with casualties.

"Pregnancy?" Harper turned to Stacy. "What pregnancy?"

"I just found out," she answered weakly.

"When were you planning to tell me?" her friend demanded. "Before or after I moved?"

Noting Cole's startled look, Stacy sank onto the couch. Why had she imagined she could keep secrets from the two people closest to her?

"I'm surprised to hear you're leaving," Cole said to Harper.

Stacy held up both hands. "Stop." Two pairs of

eyes fixed on her. "I'm not your responsibility. Either of you."

Harper's head swiveled as she made the connection between her and Cole. "He's the father?"

Stacy had forgotten that other confidential matter. *Blam* went the caboose, toppling what little remained of the train station. The only course left was to run damage control. "Don't blame him. I could have taken a morning-after pill."

Neither of them responded. They were too busy staring each other down. "Yes, I am," Cole announced. "And I'm prepared to do my share."

That had to be the most unromantic statement Stacy had ever heard. She felt like crying, which was ridiculous. Why did she keep hoping for more than the man was capable of giving?

"I can't unsign the lease, so Stace, you're moving with us," Harper said. "It's a three-bedroom house."

"I'd prefer to move here," Cole said, as calmly as if they were discussing dinner plans. "But it's up to Stacy."

Her decision became sparkling clear. "No to both of you," she answered. "I'll look for a new roommate, and if I can't find one, I'll get a smaller apartment."

"You can't live alone." Setting aside the take-out sack, Cole joined her on the couch. Earnest, concerned. *Doing his share.*

"He's right. And afterward, how are you going to manage the baby?" Harper asked. "Does Adrienne know?"

"I'm giving it up for adoption, and yes, I saw Adrienne yesterday," Stacy replied. "I'll be fine."

She wished Cole would do something other than

gaze at her in a faintly baffled way. Take her hands. Get down on his knees. Tell her he couldn't live without her.

But he wasn't that kind of man. And the sooner she dispensed with such childish fantasies, the better.

COLE ADMIRED THE RATIONAL way Stacy was handling all this. Having her roommate jump ship must have come as a shock, yet she hadn't grabbed at either of the alternatives they'd proposed.

"I'll help you find a roommate, if that's what you want," he told her. "And if you can't, I'll pay half the rent, regardless of whether you let me move in."

"That won't be necessary," she replied tautly.

"I want to." From her frown, he sensed that he was missing the point. This was more difficult than he'd expected.

Cole had done a search on the internet before coming over. He'd typed in, "What should a man do if he gets his girlfriend pregnant?" Up had popped a site labeled "What to do if your girlfriend gets pregnant: ten practical ideas." Now there, Cole had figured, was the kind of information every guy ought to have.

The suggestions had included "Act like you care," which wasn't hard, because he did. Also "listen to her" and "be honest about how you feel." But what if he wasn't sure how he felt—or rather, what if his emotions about babies were evolving, possibly in a direction that she wasn't going to like?

"Help her decide what to do"—she'd already decided that on her own. "Be there for her." He was trying, damn it. The other topics had been equally useless.

He hated seeing tears darken Stacy's eyelashes. He'd done this to her in a moment of selfishness. Why wouldn't she let him put it right?

If only she'd melt into his arms. He'd pull her onto his lap, stroke her hair and soothe away those worry lines.

Except, he admitted silently, this situation was no longer solely about him and Stacy. They had a child on the way. A little boy or girl who was going to star in somebody's cell phone pictures and fill someone's home with teddy bears and picture books.

Harper checked her watch. "I have to go. I won't be long."

"Regardless, this is not a discussion suitable for a six-year-old to hear," Stacy said. "Does she know you're moving yet?"

"Not yet," Harper admitted. "If I hadn't signed the lease and paid the first month's rent..."

"Go."

"As I said, I signed already."

"I meant, go get your daughter."

"Oh, that." Harper grabbed her purse. "See you."

When they were alone, Cole helped Stacy set the food out on the table. He'd brought several entrées, as well as salad and garlic bread, and she ate hungrily.

During dinner, he told her about the afternoon's speech and the audience reaction. She beamed at him. "You made quite an impression. Well, of course! You're one of the world's foremost experts."

"Not on reduced sperm counts," he said. "That was Dr. Tartikoff's idea."

"But you're a leader in your field." Stacy swallowed some milk before adding, "That's why people listen to you and respect you."

"Thanks." Cole hadn't expected to hear praise over the dinner table. At the only dinner table he'd regularly shared with anyone, Dr. Colette Rattigan—aka

Mom—had analyzed the day's mistakes and gone over how to rectify them.

In other words, she'd given him constructive criticism.

No wonder I've always preferred living alone.

Being with Stacy was different. Cole wanted to move in with her more than ever, now that he realized emotional support could flow in both directions.

"I hope you'll reconsider," he said as he set slices of tiramisu on plates for them. "Sharing quarters will have advantages for us both."

"Advantages?" She scowled at the layered, coffee-drenched cake. "Doesn't this have rum in it?"

Cole hadn't thought of that when he chose the rich dessert. "It's been baked. Surely there's no alcohol left."

"Flattered as I am by your reference to sharing quarters, I'll pass," Stacy said. "On the dessert, too. I already feel the size of a barn."

Pregnant women had a reputation for being touchy, Cole recalled as he downed his slice of dessert and got started on Stacy's. She didn't say anything more, and his mouth was too full to talk.

The door opened, and a little girl came bouncing in with excitement. "I'm getting a kitten!" she cried as she raced toward them. Catching sight of Cole, she paused for an instant, before she found something more worthy of her attention. "What are you eating?"

"Cake, but Cole took it all," Stacy grumbled.

Fork in hand, he hesitated over the last bite. She'd refused once. How was a man supposed to know she hadn't meant it?

Mental note: When a woman refuses dessert, ask her again.

"Sorry." He held out the plate. "If you want it..."

"She's eaten more than enough sweets for one day," Harper commented, coming through the door. "Mia, this is Dr. Rattigan."

"Oh, you're a *doctor!*" the little girl said. "Don't give me a shot, okay?"

"I won't. I promise."

That seemed to satisfy her. Nevertheless, the presence of a child created a whirlwind atmosphere in the apartment. The girl displayed small toys from a goody bag while dancing around and chattering about the birthday party. It had featured a police theme dreamed up by the birthday girl's stepmother, a former police officer. Each child had received a badge and an ID card with his or her own picture. They'd flown toy helicopters around the neighborhood while patrolling for crimes and arresting "criminals" that Harper explained were plastic golf balls painted with burglar masks.

"It was like an Easter egg hunt," Mia told them.

"What fun." Stacy gave the little girl a hug. "I'm glad you had a good time."

Feeling like the odd man out, Cole cleared the table and said goodbye. Did other men instinctively know what to say to children? Or did it get easier when you knew them better?

On the drive home—he'd brought the car this time—he sorted through his turbulent emotions. While he'd enjoyed hanging out with Stacy, he wasn't sure how to cope with her moods. Also, he experienced a touch of guilt. He shouldn't have eaten her dessert, even after she'd refused it. A gentleman would have saved it to offer to her roommate, or her roommate's child. But was it even appropriate to give sweets to a little girl who'd just filled up on birthday cake and ice cream?

He should get some practice babysitting. That would

give him a clearer idea of how one established rules and a routine. Except what would be the point, since he wasn't going to be a father other than in the genetic sense?

He wondered why he kept forgetting that fact. Was it possible he had paternal instincts?

Cole recalled reading a study that showed men's testosterone levels dropped after they became fathers. Researchers had theorized that this drop might be an evolutionary development to help men commit to their families and play a larger role in raising them by reducing aggressive behaviors. Perhaps being in the proximity of Stacy's maternal hormones was altering his body chemistry.

At home, Cole sprang up the outer stairs and stepped into his apartment, expecting his usual relief at finally being alone. Instead, he felt as if he'd entered a motel room. Aside from the electronics and the table lamp, nothing inside belonged to him. The place looked bland and impersonal.

He'd never minded before.

Cole switched on the TV. Watching the news tended to calm him. Even bad news made him appreciate his good fortune.

The screen zeroed in on a car crash, with ambulance lights flashing and firefighters struggling to free someone from the wreckage. Who was inside? Had any children been hurt?

What was with this surge of empathy? Maybe his testosterone levels really *were* dropping.

He switched channels, stopping when he came to a report of a new earthquake study. Since it dealt with probabilities and scientific projections rather than any specific event, Cole found the drone of the announcer soothing. He left the TV on while he went to change into pajamas.

From the bedroom, he heard the name Safe Harbor jump out of the broadcast, as if it were his own name. But wait, that *was* his name being pronounced—in a tone of doom.

Cole shot into the living room. There, on the screen, loomed his white-coated image on the stage of the hospital auditorium. "We hear reports from around the globe that sperm counts are dropping," he was saying. There was a quick, almost imperceptible cut, and then: "The man's condition is involved in about sixty percent of infertility cases." Followed by: "Toxins in our food, our air and our water." Another cut. "We could be in trouble."

"That was the prediction today from men's fertility expert Dr. Cole Rattigan," the anchorwoman informed viewers.

"No, it wasn't!" Cole snapped, outraged that someone had stitched his words together to create what sounded like an alarming prophecy.

Annoyed, he changed channels again. Flipping past a hamburger commercial and a man touting used cars, he landed on another newscast. "Is mankind's future in doubt?" a jowly male reporter queried from the screen. "According to Dr. Cole Rattigan of Safe Harbor Medical Center..."

Cole turned off the news. Preoccupied with his personal life, he'd put this afternoon's events out of his mind. He'd certainly never anticipated such sensationalism.

Remembering that he'd set his phone on silent mode before visiting Stacy, he scooped it up from the coffee table and checked for messages. Since the number was private, he didn't expect any calls from the press, and there weren't any. Only a message from Jennifer Martin.

"If you haven't seen the news yet, I'm sure you will," said her recorded voice. "Don't let it bother you. The media love to blow things out of proportion, and Saturdays are notoriously slow news days. By Monday they'll move on to something else." During a short pause, he thought he heard her mutter, "I hope." In a louder voice, she said, "Keep a low profile. Call me if you have any questions, and enjoy your evening."

Keep a low profile? How, exactly?

Despite his rising frustration, Cole reminded himself that there was nothing he could do about this. Anyway, compared to his concerns about Stacy and her pregnancy, this fuss struck him as the proverbial tempest in a teapot.

Mankind's ability to reproduce was not even close to being in danger. And he was the living proof.

Chapter Nine

Stacy fell deeply asleep at eight o'clock and awoke in the middle of the night with ideas buzzing in her brain. Pulling a pad from beside the bed, she began writing a notice for the bulletin board.

"Surgical nurse seeks roommate. Must be quiet, reliable, kind, funny, sweet, good in a crisis and empathetic."

She tapped the paper with her pencil. What kind of list was that? It sounded like a description of Cole, except for the empathetic part.

She wished she hadn't been so angry with him last night. Her snappishness about the tiramisu had obviously caught him off guard. True, Andrew would have plied her with dessert until he'd talked her into eating it, which was what she really wanted. But that had been in their early days.

Yet these *were* her early days with Cole. And most likely these were all the days they were going to have. No way on earth would she let him move in with her, although she appreciated his offer to pay rent.

Stacy crossed out the adjectives, jotted down the price of rent and the convenient location two miles from work, and set down the pad. She must have gone to sleep again, because the next thing she knew, morning light was filtering through the blinds.

From the living room came the blare of an animated video. High, squeaky cartoon voices didn't usually bother her, but today they set her nerves on edge.

There was a tap on the door, and Harper came in with a tray of toast and tea. "We'll be leaving for church soon. I thought you might need this."

"Thanks," Stacy said, nearly adding, "I'll miss you when you move." But she didn't want to pile any more guilt on her friend.

After positioning the tray on Stacy's lap, Harper picked up the notepad. "I'll print this up for you and do that fringe thing so they can pull off your email address."

Her mouth full of rye toast—her favorite—Stacy mumbled, "You don't have to…"

"It's no trouble. I'm glad to help." Tearing off the sheet, Harper scooted out.

"I meant…" What? That she felt reluctant to post the notice? It was the quickest way to find a roommate. Besides, she didn't *have* to accept someone just because he or she responded.

When she got out of bed half an hour later, Stacy found sections of the Sunday newspaper scattered between the living room and the kitchen. As she collected the ones that interested her, she wished she had someone there to rub her feet. Did Cole do that sort of thing?

During their courtship, Andrew had given her wonderful massages…. Why did she keep thinking about him?

Because I still don't understand why he fell out of love with me.

Figuring it out might help Stacy prevent the same

thing from happening again with a new man. Except, of course, she had yet to meet someone who'd cherish and adore her forever, and she wasn't likely to in her condition.

It seemed like a million years ago, instead of nine or ten, that she'd first seen Andrew—at a student rally at Cal State University, Long Beach. He was an impressively built guy, and he'd been surrounded by friends. Stacy had felt his gaze flick over her, but didn't believe he'd noticed her particularly.

A while later, when the crowd grew rambunctious—to this day, she couldn't remember the cause they'd been protesting—she'd lost her footing. A strong hand had grasped her arm and pulled her to safety.

When she looked up into Andrew's green eyes, she'd felt a jolt of electricity. The spark had been instantaneous and intense. The man had bowled her over, taking her to dinner, asking about her life and dreams, sharing his past as a high school football star and the difficulties of adjusting to a less exalted role as a college student in business administration.

Soon they were spending all their spare time together. Starstruck, she'd encouraged and admired him, and he'd been enthusiastic about her plans to become a surgical nurse. Andrew had a gift for making romantic gestures, for anticipating her needs and for saying the right things. Stacy had found it hard to believe she'd discovered such an ideal guy, and that he'd fallen for her.

He'd graduated a year ahead of her. Although she'd feared they might drift apart once he began working, he'd proposed. Right after her graduation, they'd had a storybook wedding.

Over the next few years, his heavy schedule of traveling for his employer and her long hours as a nurse had made it difficult to maintain their closeness. Yet just when Stacy would start to feel concerned, Andrew would surprise her with a romantic getaway or a thoughtful gift that restored her confidence. He had exquisite taste in jewelry....

She'd worried that he might meet other women when he was out of town. Her mother had advised her to trust him, warning that nothing drove a man away faster than a nagging, suspicious wife. Ironically, it wasn't some glamorous businesswoman who stole him but a former high school girlfriend who worked in town as an ultrasound technician.

Stacy had been putting in extra shifts at the hospital, since they'd agreed to start a family once their savings reached a certain level. So she hadn't realized he was seeing someone else until the evening Andrew presented her with the divorce papers. He told her he'd fallen back in love with Zora. She made him happy in a way that Stacy no longer did.

He hadn't left any room for discussion. No counseling, no attempt to save their marriage. He wanted out.

Numb with shock and pain, Stacy had agreed. She still couldn't figure out where she'd gone wrong. She missed those early years, that uplifting sense of being deeply loved and cherished. How could their bond have dissolved so completely without her realizing it?

She tried to picture Cole madly in love. All she could visualize was him crouching in the parking garage retrieving her lipstick from behind a tire. Even a casual stranger would do that.

In the kitchen, Stacy put the kettle on to boil. Closing her eyes, she inhaled the lingering scents of pesto sauce and garlic. What a delicious dinner he'd brought last night. She wished she hadn't been so rude about the dessert.

What was Cole doing this morning? she wondered.

When the tea was ready, she settled in to read the paper. On the bottom half of page one, folded so she hadn't seen it before, was a picture of Cole, his eyes keen and his lips parted as he spoke into a microphone.

Pride surged through Stacy. Then she read the headline, "Man's future in doubt? M.D. cites low sperm counts." While he'd mentioned speaking on the subject, she doubted he'd done so in such an inflammatory fashion.

The article began with the same provocative angle as the headline, but the rest sounded more like Cole: calmly informative. Stacy considered clipping it to give to him, until it occurred to her that the public relations office would no doubt secure plenty of copies.

Moving to the sports section, she saw that an Orange County gymnast was in an international competition to be aired in about ten minutes. She switched on the TV in the living room.

A newscaster was droning on about a bill scheduled to come before Congress that week. Then she heard the anchorwoman say, "If you're worried about our budget problems, here's even scarier news. In another generation or two, there might not be enough young people to pay taxes, according to a California fertility expert."

Cole appeared, broad-shouldered in his white coat as he faced the camera. "We hear reports from around the globe that sperm counts are dropping." An almost imperceptible blip was followed by: "We could be in trouble."

Back to the anchorwoman. "That's the word from

Dr. Cole Rattigan at Safe Harbor Medical Center. He cites statistics that show…"

The words blurred as Stacy realized that this was no longer a local story. It had made the network news.

Whether Cole liked it or not—and he probably hated it—anything he did was likely to be broadcast. Such as revealing that he'd impregnated his surgical nurse. That was all Stacy needed, for her parents to see her embarrassing situation played up like some cheesy reality show. Her father would be horrified. Both her reputation and Cole's would be dragged through the gossip mill.

Until this moment, she hadn't realized how much she'd been hoping that somehow, despite her protests, Cole would wind up as her new roommate. Glumly, she faced the fact that, for both their sakes, she couldn't let that happen.

"REFUSE ALL INTERVIEWS and don't post any comments online unless Jennifer or I approve them first," Owen Tartikoff warned Cole on Monday afternoon. The fertility chief, fresh from surgery judging by the strong smell of antiseptic, had stopped by Cole's office in the medical building.

"Too bad. And here I was planning to write a blog about the imminent end of the human race," Cole deadpanned.

"You may think this is funny, but the media will twist anything you say."

"They already have," Cole pointed out. He had no intention of writing or saying anything about the Daddy Crisis, as some hyperventilating reporter had called it. Somehow, even on a Sunday, the fearmongers had dredged up a few experts to comment pro and con.

Each time, the TV stations reran clips of Cole's remarks.

He clung to the hope, as Jennifer's email had suggested, that today would bring fresh news to fill their gossip-casts. Never before had Cole wished so hard for a senator to commit some deadly sin or a celebrity to get caught shoplifting.

"I'm just offering friendly advice." Owen tried his most intimidating stare on Cole. "Keep it low-key."

"You sure you don't want me to give any more lectures?" Cole asked. "How about one called 'Teach Your Sperm to Do the Conga'?"

"You're enjoying this," Owen growled.

Only the part where I'm having fun at your expense.

"If you light a fire, don't complain when it gets too hot."

"Point taken."

Nurse Luke Mendez, who went by the nickname Lucky, glanced meaningfully through the partly open door. They had a waiting room full of patients, with several prepped in examining rooms.

"I'll let you get to work." With that, Dr. T. departed, his aura of power fraying around the edges.

That day and the next, Cole arrived early and stayed late, treating more patients than usual. The publicity had inspired a flood of calls. Lucky referred many of the men to other urologists for preliminary workups. However, they tried to squeeze in those patients whose infertility had defied diagnosis.

Cole had nearly forgotten about Peter Gladstone, until Tuesday around 6:00 p.m., when he picked up the day's final chart and recognized the name of the biology teacher who'd fended off the reporters. A check of the man's records and medical history showed that his previous doctor had ruled out the usual problems. Neither his age—thirty-one—nor his medical history waved any red flags.

In the examining room, Cole shook hands with the blond teacher, exchanged pleasantries and conducted a physical exam. Normal protocol. He could double-check the other doctor's findings, but he didn't like to subject a patient to costly duplicate tests.

He also wanted to assess how Gladstone was dealing with infertility. For many men, difficulties with becoming a father delivered a serious blow to their sense of worth. Some became depressed and angry and avoided friends and relatives with children. Others tried to compensate by going overboard in their work, sports or other activities. If a patient had trouble coping, Cole referred him to counseling and to support groups such as Resolve.org.

Peter, however, seemed clear-headed and focused. Becoming a father had been important to him all his life, he explained. "My dad's been a great role model. We played sports together while I was growing up, and he's the person I turn to for advice. I always planned to have that kind of experience with my own children."

"What about adopting?" Cole asked.

"Not much chance for a single guy." The man folded his arms, emphasizing his well-developed muscles. "Also, my mother's hooked on genealogy. She's traced our family history back a couple of centuries. We've been an interesting bunch, including an inventor, a Revolutionary War hero and a buccaneer, which I guess is a pirate. My sister doesn't want kids. I hate to think the line would end with me."

"Family history can be important." Not that Cole had any personal experience with that. His mother had been adopted by a narrow-minded couple against whom she'd rebelled. As far as he knew, she'd never tried to find her biological family. He hadn't been close enough to his father for discussions about ancestry.

Irrelevant.

"You mentioned sports," he said. "Is that in your medical history?" He could only recall a reference to regular exercise.

Peter shrugged. "I'm an assistant wrestling coach, if that makes any difference."

"It might." Cole jotted a note. "You're a wrestler yourself?"

"All through high school and college," Peter confirmed.

"Ever get injured?" he asked.

The teacher chuckled. "I never met a wrestler who didn't. Bruises and strains come with the territory. Nothing severe, though. My dad insisted on proper equipment and training techniques."

"He was your wrestling coach?"

"For a while."

Cole disallowed his twinge of envy at this father-son bond. He was here to help the patient, not indulge in regrets over matters beyond his control. "Ever take a blow to the balls?"

This time, Peter laughed outright. "Is that medical terminology?"

"Sometimes it's best to be direct," Cole replied with a smile.

"Well, yes, sure." Abruptly, all mirth vanished. "Could that be what's causing this?"

"It's a remote possibility," Cole said. "Since nothing else has shown up, I'd like to test you for antibodies to your own sperm."

The teacher regarded him in bewilderment. "How is that possible?"

"Sperm is usually protected from the immune system by a mechanism called the blood-testis barrier," Cole explained. "Sometimes an injury breaks through this barrier. In that case, the immune system may form antibodies to the sperm."

"You said that was rare."

"It's found in less than one percent of infertile men," Cole agreed, "although the incidence is higher when they've had surgery on their reproductive tract. I don't see that in your case. But the wrestling might have caused it."

"This test—is it invasive?" The man swallowed. "Never mind. I'll do whatever it takes."

His determination to become a father, even without a woman in the picture yet, was striking. Although Cole tried to avoid becoming overly invested in his patients, he hoped he could help.

"We need to test a sperm sample for antibodies," he assured him. "Nothing invasive."

"Let's do it."

Cole summoned Lucky to arrange for the specimen. Then, in his office, he made notes in the patient's file. The problem was that even with a diagnosis, treatment for male antibodies was controversial and uncertain. He supposed they'd cross that bridge when and if they came to it....

A tap at the door announced an unexpected visitor. Ned Norwalk popped in, his teeth gleaming white in his tanned face when he smiled. Although they'd hung out together at the Sunbeam Saloon, this was the first time the nurse had paid him a visit. "What's up?" Cole asked.

Ned dropped into a chair. "Just making sure we're on the same page."

"About what?"

"Stacy."

Irritably, Cole recalled Ned's comment at the nightclub: *There's one I wouldn't mind getting to know better.*

"What about her?"

Ned spread his hands placatingly. "I'm looking for a place, so we discussed her ad for a roommate. When she confided that she's pregnant, I put two and two together. She refused to say anything about the father, but I saw you two leaving the club, and the timing is right."

Cole pried apart his clenched teeth to ask, "And?"

"I wanted to let you know I'll take good care of her."

Considering Ned's reputation for gossiping, Cole did not feel reassured. "You will, eh?"

The nurse hurried on. "People will assume I'm the dad, which lets you off the hook. With all this publicity, I figured you'd appreciate that."

A swell of anger nearly choked Cole. He did *not* want to be let off the hook, and he hated the idea of another man living with Stacy. "You figured wrong."

Ned regarded him uneasily. "You don't like the idea?"

"Correct," Cole muttered. Then he remembered the first lesson he'd learned about Stacy: not to control her. He struggled to moderate his tone. "I should discuss this with her. Any idea where she is?"

"I saw her on the elevator a few minutes ago. She got off on the second floor. Something about an ultrasound."

The exam wasn't scheduled for another week and a half, but there must have been a change in plans. Was she having problems? Cole sprang up so fast he banged his thigh against the edge of the desk. "I'd better go."

"Yeah. Glad we had this little talk," Ned said as Cole hurried past him. "Guess I'll find another place to live."

"Excellent plan," he snapped.

He supposed he should have been more diplomatic, and more careful about revealing his paternity. Sworn the man to secrecy, too. But right now, Cole didn't care.

He had to find Stacy.

Chapter Ten

As Stacy approached Nora Franco's office, Una stepped into the hall, the tag sticking out of her flowered maternity dress. She must have already completed the ultrasound and dressed hurriedly afterward.

Stacy wished she had arrived earlier, but she'd been at home when she received a text saying the eager mom-to-be had arranged to move up her ultrasound by a few days. "How'd it go?"

"I'm having twins!" Una cried, and twirled around in the corridor.

"That's great! Hang on a sec." Reaching out, Stacy tucked the tag into the collar. "There you go. Where's Jim?"

"Hauling a load back from Oregon." Una's husband was a long-distance truck driver. "Dr. Franco knew how anxious I was, so her nurse called about a cancellation. Jim gave the okay, and here I am. Jim was ecstatic when I told him the news. Me, too!"

"I wish I'd been there." Stacy had meant to share as many special moments as possible with her co-mom.

"Don't feel bad," Una told her. "Dr. Franco and Harper were almost as excited as I was. I did kind of hope for triplets or quads, though."

Down the hall, a staff door opened. Stacy expected to see her roommate leaving for the day. Instead, she caught a glimpse of Zora Raditch's short ginger hair and green uniform. Even after nearly three years, Stacy still felt a blast of resentment toward the woman who'd stolen her husband. At least she had the good grace to duck away in the opposite direction.

Stacy returned her attention to Una. "You don't really want to be pregnant with more than two. I sure hope I'm not." She halted, startled by what she'd blurted. If she hadn't been so distracted by seeing Zora…

"You're pregnant?" Una's eyes widened.

"I had a little accident." Boy, was that an understatement.

"How wonderful!" Her fellow mom gave her a hug. "Our kids will be brothers or sisters. When are you due?"

"February," Stacy said. "A few weeks after you."

"We might deliver at the same time," Una pointed out. "That's so sweet. The kids can grow up together."

Stacy raised her hands to stem the flow of words. "I'm planning on adoption."

Silence fell as the other woman absorbed this information. "Wait! That's even more perfect. Jim and I will adopt your baby! The more the merrier."

She would do *what?* "Una, this town is full of couples with empty arms," Stacy said with more feeling than she'd intended. "Don't be…" She nearly said "greedy," but that would be offensive and just plain mean. "Think of the expense, not to mention the exhaustion."

"People at my church will help," Una responded cheerily. "Another congregant had triplets and our women's group formed a diaper and bottle brigade. I'm sure they'd do the same for me."

No way was Stacy giving her baby to the Barkers. She resented the assumption that any child of hers automatically belonged to Una.

This is my baby.

For nine months, anyway.

Still, she understood Una's desire to have a large family. Her co-mom had been a foster child, abandoned by her father and orphaned at her mother's death. Her few relatives had been indifferent. No wonder she yearned to surround herself with love.

"It isn't a good idea," she said more gently.

"Yes, it is." Una tugged her toward the elevator. "Give the idea a chance to sink in."

Talking to Una was like swimming against a strong current. "I told you…" Stacy was saying as the doors slid open.

"We'll adopt however many babies you're carrying. Once you get used to the idea, you'll see that I'm right."

Cole was standing in the elevator, his brown eyes smoldering as he took in Una's remark and Stacy's frustrated expression. "Stacy doesn't like being pressured."

Una blinked in surprise. "I beg your pardon?"

"She told you she doesn't want you to adopt her baby," Cole said firmly. "That should end the matter."

Una's gaze flicked over the name tag on his jacket. "Dr. Rattigan. You're famous!"

"*Infamous* would be more accurate." As Stacy entered the enclosed space, he touched her arm. "Watch your step."

Una's eyes widened in understanding. "He's the dad?"

Oops. "This is private," Stacy said.

Cole didn't seem to care. He was too busy glaring at Una like a bulldog guarding its territory.

As the elevator doors closed, the mom-to-be held up her hands in surrender. "My lips are sealed. As for your baby, all I ask is that you keep me in mind if you do go through with an adoption. Oh! I have a great idea."

Stacy wasn't sure she could handle any more of Una's great ideas. "What's that?"

"I'm tired of keeping a lid on the news about my pregnancy," the other woman said. "Now that we've confirmed twins, I'll ask the hospital to hold a press conference. I mean, it *is* a first for the egg bank. That ought to take the heat off you, Dr. Rattigan. Give you both a little peace and privacy."

"That would be a welcome change," Cole conceded, his tension ebbing. "Thank you."

Stacy appreciated Una's thoughtfulness. As they reached the ground floor, she said, "I'm sorry I was touchy."

"If anybody understands about mood swings, it's me." Una patted her shoulder. "See you soon."

"You bet." Stacy was glad to stay on good terms with Una. It saddened her that, although their children would be half brothers or sisters, they'd probably never meet.

Cole walked Stacy to her car. It was becoming a tradition, she mused, and a welcome one. "I appreciate your sticking up for me. Una's enthusiasm can be hard to take."

"When I heard something about an ultrasound, I was afraid you'd run into a problem," he said.

"Una's, not mine," she said. "Why'd you think it was me?"

"Ned Norwalk mentioned it." They stopped beside

her sedan. "He came to request my approval to be your roommate."

"Why would he do that?"

"I guess since I'm the father..."

Stacy didn't bother to ask how Ned had figured that out. He had a talent for snooping. "I didn't say he could move in. As a matter of fact, I've had several inquiries."

"Good." Cole regarded her hesitantly. Strange how he could be so fierce one moment and shy the next. "I warned him off."

"That wasn't up to you." Still, Ned *had* chosen to consult Cole. And Stacy felt a twinge of appreciation. Having a protector felt kind of nice.

"If you need taking care of, I should be the one to do it," he said. "This pregnancy is as much my responsibility as yours. I should be your roommate."

Stacy touched her still-flat abdomen, keenly aware of what lay inside. Part of her longed to lean against Cole and yield to his protective instincts, but she'd learned the hard way to be cautious. "One disastrous mistake per relationship is the legal limit. And we used ours when we made this child."

"Why would living together be a mistake?" he pressed.

"Because I'm vulnerable," she said. "Have you ever been in love?"

He frowned. "Define 'been in love.'"

Oh, for pity's sake!

"If you had been, you wouldn't have to ask. It will sweep away everything else like a wildfire." She recalled her intense early months with Andrew. "You'll be consumed, delirious. Longing for the person you love. Desperate to spend your life with him or her."

Cole's shoulders drooped. "I don't think that's in my personality."

"Neither do I," Stacy said sadly. "Let's leave it at that."

As she got into her car, she wasn't sure why she felt so let down. She had to stop hoping for more than Cole was capable of giving.

Especially since some foolish part of her still yearned to nestle into his arms and stay there, safe and warm.

WHEN COLE HAD REALIZED, back in Minneapolis, that he wasn't capable of committing to his girlfriend, the discovery had bothered him only because it meant distressing Felicia. More accurately, infuriating her. She'd fired off several nasty emails that had emphasized the less-than-lovable side of her personality and made him doubly glad of his escape.

It was different with Stacy. He regretted letting her down, for his own sake as much as for hers. Why couldn't he be the kind of man who made her heart beat faster?

During the next few days, Cole's thoughts kept returning to the concept of love as a sort of hemorrhagic illness. He wondered if a modified version might be acceptable to her. Seeing Stacy lifted his spirits. He missed her when a day went by without contact. Yet he supposed the fact that he could consider the situation rationally meant he didn't meet her definition of being in love. Or, as he feared, he simply wasn't capable of it.

During surgery on Friday, Cole inquired about the roommate situation. Stacy informed him that Harper was moving out the following day, but had paid for another week's rent. Stacy hoped to have chosen one of her prime candidates by then.

From the look on her face, he judged that he wasn't in the running.

On the plus side, Cole wasn't nearly as worried anymore about how the press would react if they learned of Stacy's pregnancy, which by now had become common knowledge around the hospital. Una Barker's press conference, held the previous afternoon, had succeeded in deflecting the spotlight from him.

Owen Tartikoff had spoken enthusiastically about the egg bank's first pregnancy, and Una and her husband were a sympathetic couple. Although the announcement fell short of being earthshaking, last night's local newscasts had played up the human-interest angle.

One reporter had tried to relate the case to the alleged Daddy Crisis by asking whether Una's husband required fertility treatments. Luckily, Jim hadn't. Cycling home on Friday, Cole hoped they could lay all that nonsense to rest.

Turning into the driveway, he spotted his landlady descending the steps from his apartment, her pink bubble of hair bouncing as she moved. What had she been doing up there? Emergencies aside, she was required to alert him in advance if she needed to enter.

Cole waited for her in the driveway. "Mrs. Linden?"

She gave him a too bright smile. "Hi, there! How's it going, Doc?"

"Fine. Why were you inside my apartment?"

She tugged on a tight sweater ill-suited to a woman in her late sixties. "I was in the garage and thought I heard a noise, so I went to check."

Cole didn't believe her for a second. "What kind of noise?"

"Scurrying," she said.

"Like a rat?"

"Oh, heavens no!" She sidled toward the house. "More like a squirrel."

"How can you tell the difference?"

"You scientists certainly ask a lot of questions," she responded. "I guess that's what makes you so good at your job. You know, I think I left a pot boiling on the stove. Keep an eye out for squirrels, would you? They can be a real nuisance."

If he didn't have a lease, he'd be out of there, Cole thought grumpily as he put his bike away. While her excuse might sound plausible to an outsider, he didn't buy it.

Upstairs, he fought a growing sense of discomfort as he ate a salad. Although nothing appeared out of place, he felt invaded. While he made a point of password-protecting all his electronics and keeping his financial papers in a lockbox, he shouldn't have to.

He understood that his landlady might be bored and lonely. Nevertheless, she had no business poking through his possessions, and he didn't see how he could stay there any longer.

Considering the unpleasantness of the situation, he wished she'd given him a clear-cut reason to break the lease. Instead, if he left, he might end up forking out unaffordable payments—half of Stacy's rent, as he'd offered, along with the rent on this place and the cost of a new apartment. Despite making a respectable income, he didn't see how he could manage all that.

Cole fired up his laptop and visited a site featuring the latest bicycle accessories. He'd like to buy a cyclo-computer to track his speed and mileage. On the low end, he found one for only thirty-five bucks, but it paled in comparison to a top-of-the-line competitor that also monitored heart rate and travel time, stored favorite routes and included both map features and GPS. On the downside, it cost over five hundred dollars.

He'd never been concerned about such expenses before. Now, he had to put aside money for Stacy. Just in case.

Out of curiosity, he moved the cursor to the browser window and typed in his landlady's name, Valerie Linden.

You never knew what you might find on the internet.

A list of references popped up, mostly women who were clearly not her. Then Cole remembered seeing her middle initial on a piece of misdelivered mail. He typed in Valerie Q. Linden and added Safe Harbor for good measure.

The name of a blog jumped out: *The Neighborhood Nose.* The woman snooped and bragged about it? With disbelief, he read the title of her latest entry. "Dr. Daddy Crisis: An Inside View."

There was a picture of Cole's TV set and DVD player. Another image showed his bathroom counter with his shaver and deodorant neatly lined up, followed by a similar shot of his nearly bare kitchen counter. The only thing she hadn't run were shots inside his bureau drawers and refrigerator—maybe she was saving those for later.

Judging by the date and time, she'd posted these while he was eating dinner. The nerve…

Fury shot through Cole. It took all his restraint not to storm over to her house and order the woman to remove the pictures immediately. He wasn't sure whether this qualified as a crime, but it certainly constituted grounds for a lawsuit—not that he wanted to get involved in anything so messy.

Besides, threatening a woman could bring down the law on his own head. That was all he needed, headlines about Dr. Daddy Crisis terrorizing his landlady.

Getting a grip on his outrage, Cole read what she'd written. She described how exciting it was to rent an apartment to a famous scientist, and how she'd eagerly followed news reports about him. He found two more entries from earlier in the week, one showing the exterior of the apartment and the other featuring his bicycle, wedged next to gardening implements in the garage. Both cited his orderly habits and how he always seemed lost in thought.

She didn't stop there. The woman indulged in fantasies about what he might be thinking—how he was going to save the world, a superhero in a white coat awakening mankind to its imminent demise. While he supposed some people might view this as flattering, he found it embarrassing and unprofessional.

Coupled with the press's overheated accounts, this sort of thing could turn Cole into a laughing stock. His reputation might never live it down.

Needing to see everything she'd written about him, he scanned earlier blogs about neighborhood comings and goings. She'd avoided using names, and didn't appear to have snooped inside any other houses, confining her photos to front yards, cars and open garages. While Cole doubted the neighbors would be pleased, she didn't appear to have violated their rights.

But while she didn't mention him by name, the reference to Dr. Daddy Crisis plainly identified him, and taking pictures inside his apartment was inexcusable.

He found the number of the hospital's attorney, Tony Franco, who had urged the staff to consult him at any time if a matter might reflect negatively on the medical center.

Cole intended to get those pictures taken down—pronto—without risking getting hauled off to jail for verbally assaulting his landlady. Then he was going to move out.

He hoped, into Stacy's apartment.

Chapter Eleven

Cole wasn't sure what the attorney said to Valerie Linden on the phone, but within an hour she had removed not only the offending entries but the entire blog.

"She sounded scared to death," Tony told Cole in a call later that night. "She invited you to come to her house and look through her computer. She claims she's deleted all the JPEGs."

"She might have copies," Cole hedged. He hadn't the slightest interest in entering his landlady's home. When he'd gone inside to sign the lease, he'd nearly passed out from the smell of potpourri and perfumed candles. "However, I'm willing to take her word for it."

"She seems compliant," the attorney assured him, "and I'm sure we'd all rather keep this quiet. I'll monitor her activities on the web, though, to be safe."

"Sounds good." Cole didn't want to risk attracting more publicity with a lawsuit, plus he didn't like the idea of using a sledgehammer on a gnat. He just hoped the woman had learned her lesson, so that future tenants, as well as neighbors, would be safe.

"She agreed to let you off the hook for the lease," Tony added. "If you want to move out, she won't hassle you about the rent."

"Thanks." That didn't seem like enough, so Cole added, "You've done a terrific job."

"I'm happy to help," Tony replied cheerfully. "Need any help finding a place? I know a couple of good Realtors who handle leases."

"I already have a prospect."

And he did, Cole reflected as they ended the call. Now all he had to do was change Stacy's mind.

ON SATURDAY MORNING, Cole arrived at her apartment complex armed with two thick slices of tiramisu in a sack and an African violet in a painted pot. The overall presentation fell short of what he'd hoped for, but he'd had to wait half an hour for Papa Giovanni's to open, and that ought to count for something.

At the foot of the steps, he found his way blocked by Ned Norwalk, holding up one end of a steeply tilted sofa. Disconcerted, Cole moved out of the way as the nurse, the couch and a second man, whom Cole recognized as an orderly, reached the ground.

"Hey, Doc." The surfer was breathing hard. "You here to give Harper a hand?"

"Visiting Stacy," Cole answered.

"African violets. Nice choice," Ned remarked as the pair hauled their load toward a pickup truck parked by the sidewalk.

"Glad you approve." Cole had to admit he could benefit from some coaching on the romance front. But preferably from someone other than Ned.

He hurried upstairs, eager to talk to Stacy while the guys were occupied. He'd have preferred to call ahead, but why make it easier for her to turn him down? Still, he should have considered the awkwardness of pleading his case with an audience.

Well, she wanted to be swept away. While a sack of sliced cake and a pot of flowers might not rise to such heights, he was trying.

The door to the apartment stood open. Inside, only a few pieces of furniture remained, with boxes everywhere and a large, dusty rectangle on the carpet showing where the couch had been. Amid the mess, Harper stood with hands on hips, glaring at a small girl who mirrored her pose, staring back at her. "Mia, quit fooling around and pack the rest of your toys."

"I'm hungry!" the little girl proclaimed.

"Have an apple."

"I hate apples!"

"You love apples. Besides…" Her mother caught sight of Cole. "Dr. Rattigan. Was Stacy expecting you?"

"No," he admitted. "Is she here?"

"She's at her storage unit." Harper wiped her hands on her jeans. "Deciding what to bring over."

He'd assumed she would be home at this hour. "Will she be back soon?"

"I'm not sure." Harper blew out a sharp breath. "Do you have her cell number?"

"Yes. I'll give her a call." Cole turned to go.

"That smells great!" Mia ran over to him, her gaze trained on the sack of tiramisu.

"It's reserved for Stacy," Cole responded automatically.

"All of it?"

"Cut it out, Mia," said her mother. To Cole, she added apologetically, "I know it's only ten o'clock, but she's been up since dawn. She needs a nap, but I have to show the guys where to unload stuff at the new house."

"I could watch her," he offered impulsively. Even if Stacy didn't return promptly, Cole was curious about what babysitting involved. These days, he found children fascinating in an entirely new way.

"Would you?" Gratitude shone on her face. "Thanks so much." She caught her daughter's hand. "Mia, I want you to finish packing and then take a nap. You can use your sleeping bag. Dr. Rattigan is going to stay here. I'm counting on you to be good."

"Okay, Mommy." The little girl heaved a dramatic sigh. "I'll do my best."

Ned appeared in the doorway, with the other man right behind. "Let's grab a few more boxes and go," he said. "I promised to return the pickup truck by noon."

"Oh, my gosh!" Harper grabbed a box labeled Dinnerware. Setting down his gifts, Cole hefted another box, marked Bedroom, and followed the others to the parking lot.

A few minutes later, the truck and Harper's car were loaded and the two-vehicle caravan rolled off. From the sidewalk, Cole tried Stacy's number and was sent to voice mail.

No reception at the storage unit? Disappointed, he left a message with the basic information: At her place, babysitting. Needed to talk. That pretty much covered it. He texted her, too, for good measure.

Nearing the top of the stairs, he came face-to-face with Mia. Standing a few steps up, she met him at eye level. She had a snub nose and tangled hair a few shades lighter than her mother's.

"I finished packing," the little girl announced.

"Already?"

"It's just toys. Wanna check?"

"Sure." He followed her.

The girl trotted ahead with the swagger of a miniature teenager. Not what Cole had expected, he mused. She had attitude to spare. He'd been a timid child himself.

Inside, Mia darted into a bedroom. A large bed frame leaned against the wall. In the open closet, Cole noted an unzipped garment bag containing women's clothing and realized the child must have shared this room with her mom. He didn't blame Harper for her eagerness to move to a bigger place, although the timing hadn't been good for Stacy.

He still hoped it might prove to be good for him.

Mia pointed to a cardboard box piled with dolls, games, teddy bears and picture books. "See?" she said proudly.

The haphazard assemblage offended Cole's sense of order. The box could hold at least 50 percent more stuff, with less likelihood of damage. How did you correct a child without hurting her feelings?

He got an idea. "That's a good start," Cole said. "But I'll bet there's already plenty of air at your new home."

Her forehead wrinkled. "What do you mean?"

Cole knelt on the lint-strewn carpet, glad he'd worn jeans. He'd considered putting on a suit, but decided that might look more stilted than romantic. "See all this air?" He poked between objects. "You don't have to take that."

Mia knelt opposite him, sticking one hand between the toys. "How do I get rid of it?"

"May I show you?" Cole asked.

"Okay."

He removed the contents, and then laid the flat games on the bottom and set a couple of books in place. Mia picked up on the idea, placing additional books so neatly that he let her take over. She wedged the dolls and teddy bears on top.

"That's impressive," Cole told her, noting how much more she'd managed to fit inside.

Mia beamed. "Goodbye, air!" She raised her hands and wiggled her fingers as if the air had turned into butterflies that she was setting free.

You promised to oversee her nap.

"Where's your sleeping bag?"

She indicated the closet. "I need a snack first."

"Your mother mentioned apples."

Mia studied him shrewdly. "You don't know much about kids, do you?"

"I'm not a pediatrician, if that's what you mean." Although Cole suspected he was about to be played, he was curious to find out how this little sprite's mind worked. "So?"

"Let's make brownies." She hopped to her feet. "I'll sleep real good while they're baking."

"That isn't on the agenda," Cole protested as she flitted out the door. "Too many sweets, and besides, your mother said..."

She disappeared. For a man accustomed to instant obedience from nurses and orderlies, it was disconcerting to find his objections ignored. Well, he'd sought an education in babysitting, hadn't he?

In the kitchen, Cole found Mia taking out a box of brownie mix, a bowl and a mixer. He supposed he ought to stand firm. On the other hand, the girl appeared too excited to sleep.

"Shouldn't we be packing those things?" Cole asked.

"These are Stacy's," she explained.

"She won't mind us using them?"

"She loves brownies."

Cole made a snap decision. "Let's do it. And then you go to sleep."

"Okay," Mia responded cheerily. "I promise."

IN THE CARPORT, Stacy noted Harper's empty space. Had she removed all her stuff already?

Stacy's conscience nagged that she should have offered to help. Yet with two guys at her disposal, Harper could handle this. Besides, Stacy needed to retrieve some of her possessions to replace the things Harper had taken with her, although she planned to leave her larger pieces of furniture in storage until she'd chosen a roommate.

She lifted a box of dishes from the car's trunk. When she and Harper had combined households a couple of years ago, there'd been no room for her beloved china with its delicate flower pattern. She'd missed it.

Grasping the cut-out handles, Stacy trudged toward her unit. There was nothing wrong with either of the women who were interested in moving in with her, and she owed them a quick decision. But it wouldn't be the same. After Andrew's betrayal, Stacy had found a refuge here with her old friend. Now she expected the apartment would be more of a way station than a home.

Oh, stop feeling sorry for yourself.

Stacy stamped up the steps, wincing as dishes clinked despite her careful cushioning job.

You'll survive. But if you aren't careful, your china might not.

Balancing the box on her hip, she reached for the door. To her surprise, the knob turned to reveal Cole, his hair mussed and a smudge of what appeared to be chocolate on one cheek. From inside came the unmistakable scent of freshly baked brownies.

Seeing him gave her an unexpected feeling of rightness. As though he belonged there. "What's going on?"

"You should check your phone messages." Relieving her of the box, Cole carted it into the kitchen. "I told you I was here. I assumed you'd be home, and when your roommate left, I figured I'd wait."

Stacy spotted her mixing bowl, beaters and a few utensils, freshly washed and set out to dry on the drainage board. On the counter, the timer indicated fifteen minutes remaining for the treats baking in the oven. "What's all this?"

"I'm babysitting Mia so Harper can concentrate on moving," he said, keeping his voice low. "I hope we didn't wake her."

"She's asleep?" Stacy matched his tone.

He nodded toward Harper and Mia's bedroom. "Like a dog."

"You mean a log." At six, the little girl rarely took naps anymore. "How'd you manage that?"

He smiled. "I let her con me into baking brownies and it wore her out."

Stacy laughed softly. "You're into baking now?"

"She did most of the work," Cole told her. "I had no idea children could be so skillful."

"She loves to bake." He didn't seem aware that flecks of chocolate adorned a nearby cabinet and a patch of wall, as well as his face. Dampening a paper towel, Stacy reached over and rubbed the chocolate from his cheek. "You forgot to scrub, Doctor."

Cole's gaze held hers. "Thank you, Nurse."

A delicious tremor ran through Stacy. Except for strictly professional pre-op assistance, she hadn't touched Cole since they'd made love. She shifted toward him, fascinated by his parted lips, his welcoming air. He took a deep breath, his muscles tightening as he reached to draw her close.

Recovering her senses, Stacy moved away. On the table, she noticed a sack with the Papa Giovanni's logo, and an African violet. "What's this?"

Though he looked a bit disappointed, he took her deflection courteously. "Housewarming gifts."

"Harper's the one with the new home," she said.

"You're moving, too, in a way." Cole lifted the lid from her box of dishes. "You packed them in towels. Clever."

"I heard something clink on the way up." Gently, Stacy removed a plate from its terry-cloth wrap. She didn't see any chips and put the dish by the sink.

"I'll wash them," Cole offered. "If that's what you were planning."

"There's a dishwasher." She returned to fold the towel. Since it looked clean, she decided to skip running extra laundry.

"I don't mind helping." He sucked in another deep breath. "Stacy, we need to talk."

She had a good idea of what came next. "I can't let you move in. It won't work."

He didn't ask why. Instead, he startled her by saying, "I have to leave my place."

"What's wrong with it?"

"Nothing, except that my landlady snooped in my apartment and posted photos of it on her blog."

"She did what?" Anger flared on his behalf. "That's terrible."

"Tony Franco set her straight," Cole replied. "While I doubt she'd pull the same stunt again, I don't feel comfortable staying there."

"No kidding!"

He set the next plate by the sink and folded the towel. "Have you picked a roommate?"

"Not yet." She nearly added that she had several strong candidates, but why bother? If she'd found someone ideal, she'd have chosen already, and he knew it.

"I'm not a big believer in fate," Cole commented as he continued to unpack her dishes. "But when circumstances nudge you in a logical direction, why ignore it? While you're carrying our child, Stacy, you deserve to have someone here who'll take care of you. There's an empty bedroom and I need to rent a new place."

"People will find out." Although it wasn't the main issue, it was the first objection that sprang to mind.

"Who cares?" He folded another towel.

"You should."

"But I don't. Besides, most of the staff know already."

She felt herself weakening. Cole *had* been supportive and kind. If only she didn't run the risk—in her hormone-fueled state—of falling in love with him. And then there was the question of the baby's future.

"You aren't changing my mind," she said.

Hurt shadowed his face. "Why not try it for a few months? See how it goes."

He'd misunderstood. "I meant the baby. Giving it up. There's a couple meant to have this child, and it will be a privilege to fulfill their dreams."

Face averted, he retrieved a cup and saucer. "Okay." The sadness in his voice knifed through her.

Stacy wished he'd argue with her, because that would make it easier to resist. Determinedly, she rallied her defenses. "And even though we had sex, you aren't my boyfriend." The word sounded childish, applied to this distinguished man, so she amended, “Or whatever.”

“You already declined to marry me,” Cole reminded her. Onto the counter went a salad plate. “I get the message.”

She’d never met anyone so opaque. Usually, she picked up people’s emotional states easily.

But then, Cole’s reticent personality *was* the problem. He cared, but not madly and deeply. Still, his good qualities—his honesty and dependability—suited her needs during the difficult months ahead.

“Ground rules,” Stacy ventured.

Cole studied her, revealing nothing of his emotions. “Yes?”

“We’d be friends, nothing more,” she said. “Like Harper and me.”

“Check.”

Although she’d have appreciated more discussion, he *had* conceded the point. “This doesn’t change our relationship at work.”

“Agreed.”

“No trying to influence my choices.” She was gaining momentum.

“Got that.”

“We lead separate lives,” Stacy went on. “If I choose to go out with people, or…” She had no interest in dating while she was pregnant. “…or whatever, that’s my business.”

Cole nodded. Watching her. Waiting for more terms?

Tell me you can’t live that close to me and not treasure and love and hold me....

“And after the baby’s born, once I’m on my feet again, you’ll find another place.”

"Or we renegotiate," he said. "If the arrangement suits us both, why rock the boat?"

The arrangement. Sometimes Stacy thought he chose his words specifically to frustrate her. Speaking of rocking boats, she had an impulse to tip this one and dump Cole into cold water.

If only he'd get angry. Not that she really wanted that, but she longed for an emotional reaction. For him to have fallen in love with her. But that wasn't Cole.

"We'll see," she conceded.

"I'll move in tomorrow," he said.

Wait. She hadn't exactly decided to give him permission. Yet he'd agreed to all her terms, which made it too late to back out.

Thank goodness, Stacy thought, and refused to examine her sudden rush of happiness.

Chapter Twelve

Cole didn't believe he had any expectations—hopes, perhaps, but not expectations—about what might happen between him and Stacy after they became roommates. So why, he wondered on Monday a little over a week later, did he feel so let down?

The physical process of moving in had gone smoothly. He'd hired a cleaning service, which Stacy had appreciated, as well as a moving company to bring his few possessions and her furniture from storage. Since he had only his electronics and one lamp, there'd been no problem fitting everything into their common space. For his room, Cole had ordered a bed and bureau, which arrived in timely fashion.

This past weekend, he'd purchased bedding and paid the apartment manager a small extra sum for a key to the complex's utility room, which had space for his bike. Overall, Cole should have felt completely satisfied.

And yet…

He barely saw Stacy in the mornings. She refused to let him bring her tea and toast in bed, preferring to keep crackers in her room to stave off morning sickness. Then, while she claimed she didn't mind his habit of watching cartoons during breakfast, she downed her cereal quickly and disappeared into her bathroom.

They drove to and from work separately. Her schedule ended earlier than his, and she either ate dinner at the hospital cafeteria or consumed a salad at home, finishing up by the time he arrived. In the evenings, she avoided him, or so it seemed to Cole. After he finished working on his laptop and emerged into the living room, she vanished into her bedroom, claiming she wanted to read and go to sleep early.

Under other circumstances, he'd have considered her an ideal roommate. Instead, he missed her. They were leading disconnected lives, and even though he'd agreed to her terms, surely there had to be a middle ground.

Now he restlessly finished entering notes into his office computer about the evening's next-to-last patient. The publicity surrounding him might have faded, but the residual effect was an increase in physicians' referrals and direct patient requests to see him. Trying to accommodate as many people as possible meant staying later and seeing even less of Stacy.

It was nearly seven o'clock. Although the cafeteria had delivered sandwiches several hours ago, he was getting hungry again. Still, scanning his next patient's report pushed everything else out of Cole's mind, and he hurried into the examining room.

Peter Gladstone rose to shake hands. The teacher had come for a report on his antibody test, and while the results did provide an explanation for his infertility, they offered no easy solution.

"It's positive," Cole told him.

"What does that mean, exactly?" Arms folded, the man leaned against the wall.

Cole remained standing, too. "As I explained before, men can develop an allergy to their own sperm. This may interfere with fertility in several ways." He went into detail about how sperm, under attack by the immune system, failed to fulfill their function.

Judging by Peter's expression, he had no difficulty following the medical terminology. Once Cole finished, his patient zeroed in on the central issue. "Can you fix this?"

Here came the bad news. "The treatment is to administer corticosteroids, which have dangerous, sometimes fatal, side effects," Cole said. "Among other things, they may cause a condition called aseptic necrosis, which can destroy the patient's hip, requiring replacement. I don't recommend this. You're a healthy young man. It goes against the grain to put you at serious risk for a condition that poses no threat."

The teacher sank into a chair with an air of misery. "That's it, then? I can't ever be a dad, biologically?"

"I didn't say that." Modern technology provided options. "It is possible to achieve a pregnancy through in vitro fertilization. If you are contemplating marriage, perhaps we should include your significant other in this discussion."

Peter shook his head. "Frankly, the more I think about it, the less interested I am in remarrying. Angela was the love of my life. What we shared I can never hope to find again. To bring another woman into this situation would be wrong, especially in light of my condition. So I was wondering about hiring a surrogate."

"In that case, you'd be using IVF anyway," Cole pointed out. "As you might imagine, these are expensive procedures. Safe Harbor has a grant program called the Building Families Fund, if you'd like to put in an application. I should warn you that it's highly competitive."

Peter waved away the concern. "Angela had life insurance. I can't think of a better use for it than to have children. I only wish I were having them with her."

Cole gave him a pair of brochures from the hospital's fertility program. "These will tell you more about surrogacy and IVF."

"It isn't just a medical issue, though, is it?" Peter held on to the material without glancing at it. "What if the surrogate changes her mind and wants to keep the baby? I couldn't bear to go through all this and then lose my child, or have to share custody with a stranger."

"Usually, courts uphold surrogacy contracts." Cole was glad Tony kept the staff advised about legal ramifications. "To be on the safe side, however, some parents use eggs donated by a second woman. That way, the surrogate isn't carrying her own child, which means she has no legal rights."

For the first time since receiving his bad news, Peter smiled. "How high tech is that? Wow. I like it."

"The hospital's financial counselor can help you project costs." Cole gave him the woman's card. "There's no rush. After consideration, you may prefer to pursue adopting an older child."

"I doubt it," Peter said, but tucked the card into his wallet anyway. "Thanks for pinpointing my diagnosis. Now I know where I stand."

They shook hands. Watching the teacher leave, Cole wished he could do more.

On top of everything else, how devastating for Peter to have lost the love of his life. Making notes on his computer, Cole wondered if he dared apply that term to Stacy. He'd never cared about a woman this way before. But she didn't return his feelings, and he had to accept that.

Or did he?

Friends and roommates didn't have to avoid each other. Since he'd brought his car today so he could buy groceries on the way home, Cole decided to rent a few DVDs and stock up on microwave popcorn.

Stacy might be able to resist him, but in his opinion, the smell of popcorn was irresistible.

"I NEVER FIGURED YOU for the manipulative type," Stacy said. She'd followed her nose into the living room and found Cole relaxing on her couch with a big bowl of tantalizing popcorn. He'd also rented two romantic comedies she'd mentioned wanting to see.

"I'm not manipulative," he responded cheerfully. "Mildly subversive, perhaps. But friends share things, right?"

"I guess so." How could this be the same man who, that very morning, had coolly allowed her to assist him in gowning for surgery? Who'd maintained a professional distance throughout two operations, and had, so far, kept their living arrangements private from the increasingly inquisitive staff?

Now, legs stretched out and feet propped on the coffee table, he grinned at her audaciously. "You'll note that I spread a sheet on the couch so we don't drop any kernels between the cushions. I also took off my shoes so they won't scuff the coffee table."

She'd be willing to bet he'd put on clean socks, too. Oh, for heaven's sake, what was wrong with trying to please her? "Good, thanks. So which one should we watch first?"

He let her choose.

By ten o'clock, she was too sleepy for a second movie. But with the popcorn long gone, she wasn't too sleepy to share some of the ice cream with which Cole had filled the freezer. Despite his having taken over most of that compartment, she couldn't complain about his habits, since he kept his food neatly packed into his agreed-upon half of the fridge. The cartoons he watched during breakfast grated on her nerves, but when she bothered to watch, she had to admit they *were* kind of funny.

They ate on the sofa. "My dad used to have a fit if I took food into the living room," she said. "He's way fussier than my mom."

"What does your father do?" Cole asked.

"He's a pharmacist." They'd never discussed *his* father, she realized. "What about yours?"

"He's an art curator."

"Present tense?" That surprised her. "He's still alive?"

"Last I heard." He wiggled his toes on the coffee table. "In Paris."

"You aren't close?"

Cole released a long breath. "No. That was part of the deal."

"You mean like a custody agreement?" Stacy asked.

"Not in the usual sense. He only fathered me because my mother talked him into it." He explained that his powerhouse mother had met his dad through friends. She'd chosen an art curator, on loan to a museum in Minneapolis, as an ideal father, due to his distinguished intellect and the fact that he'd soon be leaving the country. With the aid of a few bottles of wine, she'd persuaded him to sire her child.

Despite Cole's casual tone, Stacy thought she detected a note of sadness. As she listened to his account of growing up without a father, and of his failed attempt to forge a bond with the man, her heart constricted.

She understood why he'd offered to marry her and raise their child together, even though the pregnancy had been an accident. He didn't want to repeat his father's remiss behavior. Cole might even hope to redeem his lonely childhood by being a good parent.

It was admirable, though unrealistic. Stacy also recognized how little experience he had with a loving, stable marriage. Never having seen one in action, he assumed that goodwill and companionship were enough.

What a polar opposite from the Layne family. Her father remained a romantic in his sixties, bringing home flowers, buying her mother jewelry and whisking her away on a surprise Hawaiian vacation not long ago. Once, when her mom had been inexplicably grumpy, Stacy had heard her father tell her he couldn't live without her, that she was the center of his life.

"It must have been tough not having a dad." After setting her dish on the coffee table, Stacy rested her head on Cole's shoulder.

"It was the only kind of upbringing I knew," he said. "Yours was more normal, I gather."

"My family's really close," she murmured sleepily. "I thought I had that kind of marriage, but Andrew fell in love with someone else."

"Your husband must have been crazy," Cole said.

She would have hugged him for that, if she'd been sitting at a different angle. "I thought we were soul mates." Her voice caught. Wouldn't the pain ever go away? "I still don't understand what he found in Zora that he didn't have with me."

"He should have tried harder to stay in love with you."

"It doesn't work that way." Stacy sighed. "Love is the most powerful force in the world."

"And we're poor, helpless saps?" Cole clicked his tongue. "He must be a wimp."

"Andrew? He was a football player!"

"I'm not impressed with his staying power," Cole said. "By the way, what do your parents think about you being pregnant?"

The sudden shift in subject caught Stacy off guard. Lifting her head, which in her sleepy state seemed to weigh a hundred pounds, she admitted, "I haven't told them."

"Why not?"

She sat up wearily. "I'm too embarrassed."

"I thought you were close."

Good point. Now that Cole put it to her, Stacy saw how foolish she'd been. Her parents loved her. If she had a daughter who was dealing with a situation like this, she'd want to know.

"I should tell them," she said. "But not tonight." Not only was she worn out, but also, Stacy recalled guiltily, she'd promised to help Adrienne organize a housewarming party for Harper next Saturday. She still needed to respond to Adrienne's last email on the subject. "Thanks for the movie and popcorn."

"My pleasure."

She retreated to her bedroom. After emailing Adrienne about their plans, she barely mustered the energy to brush her teeth and fall into bed.

Between combating her queasiness and getting ready for the party, Stacy didn't get around to calling her mother until Thursday. Her ultrasound was scheduled for the next day, and she'd rather get the phone call over with before she had any more complicated news to report.

It shouldn't be hard, she reflected as she prepared to call her mother's cell. But Stacy had always been the one to whom other family members turned for support. She hated unloading problems on *them*.

Now, she listened to the phone ring. Four-thirty here meant five-thirty in Utah. Realizing she might be interrupting dinner preparations, she was about to cancel the call when her mother's voice said, "Stacy? Hi."

"Hi, Mom." In the background, Stacy heard a woman ask about shipping a purchase. "You're at the boutique?"

"We've been incredibly busy." Her mother sounded frazzled. "Lots of tourists this month. How are you?"

"Maybe this isn't a good time to talk." She hated to drop bombshell news on her mom while a customer waited for attention. "You're busy."

"Your sister can handle the counter. Hold on." Judging by the sounds, Ellen was moving. Then a door clicked shut, cutting off the hum of voices.

"Seriously, Mom, we can talk tomorrow. No, Saturday," Stacy corrected, remembering the ultrasound.

"This must be important, or you wouldn't be so nervous," her mother said. "Talk to me."

No getting around it. "Okay," Stacy said. "I'm pregnant."

There was a moment of silence and then her mother asked, "Are you getting married?"

"No." Out tumbled the explanation. A man she knew from work. Watching a movie and falling asleep on his couch. Poor judgment.

She winced as she pictured the frown on her mother's face and a veined hand agitatedly pushing back a shock of graying hair. Her sister had urged them to use Skype so they could see each other. Right now, Stacy was immeasurably glad they hadn't.

"This Dr. Rattigan," her mother said at last. "How did he react?"

"He asked me to marry him," she admitted. "I said no. We aren't in love. He's a nice guy and he's helping me, but I've decided on adoption."

She waited tensely. Hoping for support, bracing for criticism.

"Are you sure?" Ellen probed. "I realize Andrew hurt you badly. Don't let that sour you on marriage altogether."

"That isn't the case," Stacy assured her. "Adoption is simply the right choice."

"Then let's keep this between us," her mother said. "If you're going to give it up, there's no reason to tell your father."

What an odd reaction. Although Stacy's father could be quick to judge, it seemed strange for her mother to keep such a major secret. "Don't you two share everything?"

Ellen's quick release of breath was almost a snort. "Your father, like most men, has to be managed."

"He does?" In view of her mom's mood swings, Stacy had always thought of their father as the steady one.

"Surely you've noticed that he tends to overreact."

"Well, sometimes." During her sister's rebellious phase in high school, a bad report card had sent their father into a tightly controlled rage. He'd grounded Ellie, Jr. for a month and forced her to drop out of cheerleading. Later, he'd apologized, but by then she'd been replaced on the squad. "You really don't think I should tell him?"

"Let me give it some thought." Her mother was backing off a little. "You kind of sprung this on me."

"I'm sorry."

"I'm glad you told me, even if it did come out of the blue," Ellen replied. "It's just that you were always the peacemaker. You helped me with your dad."

If I'm such a peacemaker, why couldn't I save my marriage? But that was a question Stacy didn't expect her mother to answer. "I'll follow your advice, whatever you decide."

"You sure you're all right?" Ellen pressed. "Getting good medical care and everything?"

"Absolutely. Mom, I'm a nurse. I work at a hospital."

"There's an old saying about the shoemaker's children going barefoot," her mother warned.

"Adrienne's treating me." She'd introduced her parents to her friends when they'd visited the previous year. "I'm in excellent hands. Now go back to your customers."

"Well, okay. I love you."

"I love you, too, Mom."

Only after she clicked off did Stacy realize she hadn't mentioned the ultrasound. But what would be the point?

There was no sense worrying about what it might reveal. She'd already given her mom plenty to think about.

Chapter Thirteen

All day Friday, Stacy tried not to think about the ultrasound. She tried to avoid thinking about it while assisting Cole in two surgeries, and later while working with obstetrician Zack Sargent as he reversed a patient's tubal ligation so she could conceive a child with her new husband.

Luckily for Stacy's concentration, the conversation in the operating room focused on the egg bank, where activity was booming. News of Una's pregnancy had brought in new infertility patients and donors.

"The program is growing faster than Jan expected," observed Zack. Being married to the director dovetailed with his interest in helping infertile women. "It's exciting."

Aware that other members of the surgical team were watching her reaction, Stacy merely nodded. Everyone seemed to know that she'd become a donor and then gotten pregnant during her first cycle. But while most people had a good idea who the father was, the gossip remained discreet. Even the anesthesiologist was keeping his sharp tongue in check, since Cole had responded to a few of his comments with quelling sarcasm.

She ventured to ask, "How many pregnancies has the egg bank achieved so far?"

"Three more confirmed," Zack replied.

Rod waggled his eyebrows as he tracked the patient's vitals. Regardless of what he might be implying, Stacy was glad he didn't cite her as an unannounced statistic. Anyway, she wasn't a recipient, so she didn't count.

"How's the success rate?" After all, it wasn't the total number of pregnancies that mattered as much as how they compared to the number of implantations.

"Excellent," the surgeon responded. "Of course, since we haven't had any deliveries yet, it's too soon to congratulate ourselves."

Nevertheless, this was promising news for the program and the families involved. Under other circumstances, Stacy would have felt a swell of pride. Instead, she merely felt swollen. Although she doubted others—aside from some of the obstetrical nurses—could see her weight gain yet, she'd added a few pounds already.

It might be partly due to the ice cream she'd consumed. And the popcorn.

At three-thirty, Stacy finished her shift and went home for a nap. The ultrasound was scheduled for five forty-five. Cole had promised to arrive there as early as possible. However, since Stacy understood how often doctors ran late, she wasn't surprised to find only Eva waiting for her at Adrienne's office.

"The tech scheduled for tonight got sick," the other nurse explained as she showed Stacy to an examining room.

"Don't tell me we have to postpone." That would be a huge letdown. Why hadn't they called?

"Dr. Cavill said it's important to proceed as planned."

Eva handed Stacy a hospital-type gown. "Leave this open in the front."

"Then who…" Stacy didn't bother to hide her reaction as she realized who would be performing the scan. "Not Zora!"

Eva pushed her thick glasses higher on her nose. "Sorry. It's the best we could do."

Stacy understood the predicament. Still, the prospect of being touched by the woman made her skin crawl. Zora was sleeping with Stacy's ex-husband and had probably started sleeping with him while they were still married. In a perfect world, the woman would have to wear a big red *A* for *adulteress* on her chest.

You're a nurse. Get over it.

Gritting her teeth, Stacy changed clothes, pressed the ready button and sat on the examining table. Zora must have been waiting outside, because a knock sounded instantly, and the tech entered with the ultrasound equipment on a wheeled cart. After a hasty nod, the green-clad technician began plugging in and setting up for the scan.

Although Stacy caught annoyingly frequent glimpses of Zora around the hospital, she didn't recall ever being alone in the same room with her. At close range, she could smell the other woman's light floral fragrance and, this late in the day, a hint of perspiration. As hard as Stacy tried to ignore Zora, she kept noticing details: her reddish-brown hair, shorter and curlier than Stacy's. Her rather thin face. Her unspectacular figure. What on earth did Andrew see in her that had been lacking in Stacy?

Having finished her initial tasks, Zora gave Stacy an apologetic glance. "I was the only tech available."

"I heard." She pressed her lips together.

"And at a time like this…" Zora swallowed. "I realize how upset you must be."

Why should Zora care? "It's not that big a deal," Stacy muttered. "It's just an ultrasound."

"I meant, Andrew told me how strongly you didn't want children." The woman squeezed gel onto Stacy's abdomen. "Sorry if this feels cold."

Stacy was too stunned by her statement to care about the gel. "He told you *what?*"

"The reason you split up." The tech sounded bewildered. "Because you didn't want kids."

"You have to be joking!" Stacy snapped. "We were planning to start a family as soon as we saved enough money."

The other woman paled. "That's not what he…told me." She seemed to run out of breath.

Had Zora not been so obviously shaken, Stacy might have believed she was faking. "Either you misunderstood or he lied."

"I couldn't have," Zora responded. "Is it possible *he* misunderstood?"

"Not in a million years."

A tap at the door cut her off. It was Cole, his expression eager. "I'm not late, am I?"

Stacy tried to give him a welcoming smile, but her cheek muscles had gone numb.

"We were just starting, Dr. Rattigan," Zora told him, and bent to her work.

Stacy wanted to focus on this moment, when she was about to see her baby or babies for the first time, but Zora's statement had shaken her. Why had Andrew lied to the woman he'd fallen in love with? What kind of basis was that for a marriage?

There was no way to make sense of this. Not that

she could figure it out, however hard she tried. Perhaps once it all sank in, she'd gain perspective. She hoped so.

As the sensing device moved across her stomach, Stacy turned her attention to the monitor.

STACY AND THE TECHNICIAN kept their gazes averted as if he'd interrupted something. Cole folded his arms, wishing he understood the vibrations in the room.

Once, during college, he'd stopped by a female friend's dorm room to lend her his study notes, and interrupted an all-girl gathering. Four flushed faces had regarded him with varying degrees of discomfort. Later, his friend had explained that they were playing a game called Truth or Dare, which apparently consisted of them revealing embarrassing secrets.

Cole didn't see the point of baring one's soul for the entertainment of one's friends. True, last Monday he'd told Stacy about his parents' unorthodox arrangement, but that hadn't been a game. Anyway, he doubted she and the ultrasound tech had chosen this particular moment to exchange confidences. He must be projecting his own mixture of excitement and concern onto the women.

The technician, whose name tag read Z. Raditch, was moving the paddle across Stacy's abdomen while adjusting knobs on the monitor. "Isn't that a heartbeat right there?" Cole asked, and pointed.

"Yes, Doctor." She cleared her throat. "It's nice and steady."

One down. His pulse quickened.

Stacy was staring at the screen, her expression unreadable. How did she feel, seeing her baby? As breathless as he did?

Even though at this early stage it appeared as a

squiggly shape with a heart throbbing in the middle, everything was there. Cole knew that the eyes and limb buds were starting to form, and within a few weeks the nose and ears would become visible. Arms would grow and bend, and there'd be tiny toes appearing on the feet. Internally, the organs were taking shape, obeying their genetic instructions.

It was nothing short of miraculous. And to him, despite all his training and experience, a revelation.

"I see another one." The technician indicated a second sac, its tiny heart throbbing like the first.

"Twins." Stacy's voice trembled.

Two children. Cole grasped her hand. Stacy squeezed his in return.

Behind him, he felt the air stir as someone entered. From the corner of his eye, he glimpsed Adrienne's white coat and blond hair.

His instinct told him to move aside, since this was her patient. Then he remembered that, rather than being a consulting physician, he was the dad.

Cole's throat tightened. These tiny, pulsating blobs of humanity had a grandfather in Paris and a grandmother who'd forged her own path as a surgeon. *And they might never know.*

"Oh, my word!" The paddle gave a jerk, and the technician had to stabilize it. "There's a third one."

"Triplets." Stacy shivered.

"You okay?" Cole asked, his feeling of awe mutating into unease. A multiple pregnancy often meant serious health hazards.

She lay there stiffly. "I guess."

"Let's make sure there aren't any more," Adrienne said.

"Yes, Doctor," responded the tech.

Several tense minutes passed as the sensing device made additional passes. Once, Cole thought he spotted a fourth sac, but it turned out to be one of the original three.

He heard Adrienne's breath of relief. "Three are more than I'd like to see, but it could have been worse. I mean—well, you know what I mean. The more babies, the greater the risk."

"It's manageable, though," he said. "Given her general good health."

Adrienne quirked an eyebrow. Had he come across as too clinical?

"A positive attitude benefits the patient," Cole added.

"You're right," Adrienne conceded. "You'll do great, Stacy."

She didn't answer.

The tech cleaned the goo from Stacy's stomach and retreated from the room, wheeling her cart out. The name Raditch finally sank in. That was the director of nursing's last name, so this must be her daughter. Only she'd been wearing a wedding ring—that meant daughter-in-law.

While Cole tried not to listen to rumors, he'd heard enough to make the connection. No wonder Stacy seemed unusually tense. This was the Jezebel who'd destroyed her marriage.

After Stacy got dressed, the three of them lingered while Adrienne previewed what lay ahead. Extra testing, including a second ultrasound in a few weeks, and the possibility of bed rest or hospitalization late in the pregnancy. Stacy listened, asking few questions. As a nurse, she probably could have delivered the spiel herself.

Finally, she said, "I guess this will make some family very happy."

You can't mean that.

Surely she didn't intend to go through this difficult, dangerous process, to usher three beautiful babies into the world, and then give them away.

Cole held his reaction in check. He'd promised not to interfere. But it was killing him.

With the medical session finished, Adrienne and Stacy reviewed their plans for tomorrow afternoon's housewarming party. Stacy would be fixing some of the food, while Adrienne was preparing the flower beds at Harper and Mia's new home for plants. They'd suggested those as gifts on the email invitation.

At last Adrienne shook hands with the two of them. "I have other patients waiting. We'll keep a close watch on this pregnancy. I'm sure it will turn out fine."

"Let me know if there's anything I can provide, beyond the obvious," Cole interjected.

"You bet."

Despite his offer of a ride, Stacy insisted on driving herself home. As she pointed out, she'd brought her car, and she claimed that she was handling the earthshaking news just fine.

"Pregnancy didn't turn me into a china doll," she assured him.

"Well, it's turning me into a worrywart," he answered.

Stacy gave him a hug. "And a cute one."

That made him feel better. Still, he wished she'd accept his support.

Once he'd seen her off at the parking structure, Cole meandered back into the hospital. The cafeteria's advertised special tonight was Better Than Your Mother's Meat Loaf. Since Colette Rattigan's meat loaf had come frozen from the store, he was curious to find out how this tasted.

Passing the day care center, Cole halted as Owen Tartikoff barreled through the door, a toddler tugging on each hand. "Sorry," the fertility chief told Cole with a grin. "They're hungry."

"Guess their mom's got dinner ready, huh?" he asked wistfully.

"No, she's at choir practice." The tall man nearly lost his balance as the twins yanked him forward. "We're eating at the cafeteria. Care to join us? I'm kidding. Nobody in his right mind would volunteer for this."

"That's okay." Cole fell into step beside them. "I'm tired of eating alone."

The twins' dueling cries of "Da-Da!" and "Hungwy!" filled him with a sense of wonder. When he'd arrived at Safe Harbor last summer, they'd been five-month-old babies squawking and babbling in a double carriage. Now they were chatty toddlers.

As they sat around a table, Cole noted that the boy had red hair like his father, and the girl medium brown curls like her mother. He'd heard the boy had been named Richard after the composer Richard Rodgers, and the girl Julie after the heroine of the Rodgers and Hammerstein musical *Carousel.*

Who would name the triplets? Cole wondered.

Quit torturing yourself. He returned his attention to the kids.

Julie was taking tiny spoonfuls, careful to avoid dropping a single kernel of corn. Richard milled his food into a big pile and was barely prevented from plopping his face into it by his father's outstretched arm.

I want to hear my kids call me Da-Da. I want to

know when to stick out my arm to keep my babies from getting a snootful of mashed potatoes.

Cole had to change Stacy's mind, not only about the kids but about him. Since she yearned to be swept away, he decided to start researching how men accomplished that. "How did you propose to your wife?" he asked.

"Beg pardon?" Owen plucked a green bean out of Richard's hair.

"Did you just ask her? Did you get down on one knee? Or did you do something fancy?"

"All of the above. Hang on." The chief won a staring contest with his son, who finally settled down to eat. "I sang 'You'll Never Walk Alone' from *Carousel.* Then I got down on my knee and begged her to marry me."

Cole could see how a woman might enjoy that. While he had the voice of a lonely frog, some sort of private performance might be feasible. "Did you stage this anywhere in particular?"

"In the hospital auditorium in front of a few hundred people," Owen said. "I'm surprised no one's mentioned it to you."

"All I heard was that you fell in love with a nurse." Initially, when Owen offered him a job at Safe Harbor, Cole had hesitated to accept because of the surgeon's reputation for harshness. Learning that the man wasn't such an ogre had changed his mind. "People said you'd turned romantic. But no details."

"Now you know."

"Interesting." Unfortunately, it didn't help Cole's situation. If he ever sang in public, people would likely throw shoes at him.

Realizing he was neglecting his meat loaf, he took a bite, deciding he hadn't missed much by eating the frozen variety.

As for Stacy, Cole doubted he'd win her over by doing something melodramatic and against his nature. He'd just have to watch for a chance to sweep her away that didn't involve humiliating them both in public.

Chapter Fourteen

Stacy awoke Saturday morning feeling as if she'd fought ten rounds of a boxing match. All night her brain had hopped from topic to topic, while her hormones demanded sleep.

The result had been a series of disturbing dreams. As the morning sunlight peeked into the bedroom, she recalled wispy fragments. Andrew earnestly presenting her with a jeweler's box, which she opened to reveal a heap of bronzed baby booties. Zora wielding the ultrasound paddle like a hot iron. Cole talking to her with no words coming out. Why couldn't she understand him?

Still, she'd received a couple of shocks yesterday. Three babies. Her hand instinctively cupped her stomach. Pregnancy in triplicate. And then there was what Zora had said about Andrew.

He hadn't simply been overwhelmed by love. A man who adored and cherished a woman didn't lie to her. Well, not an honorable man, anyway. Of course, an honorable man didn't cheat on his wife, either.

Yet the man Stacy had fallen in love with in her college days had been golden to her. Larger than life, charismatic, warm, tender. Why and how had he changed?

Restlessly, she went about preparing for the day.

The housewarming party started at three o'clock, and although Harper had arranged for a caterer to deliver the main dishes a little later, Stacy had promised to fix hors d'oeuvres to feed early arrivals. She was also making a special dessert: two Boston cream pies. Mia had requested them at the urging of her friend Fiona, who used to live in Boston.

Why on earth did I agree?

Stacy studied the recipe she'd downloaded. This wasn't a simple cake. It had layers, a cream filling and chocolate sauce.

Better get started.

Off she went to the supermarket to buy the ingredients. All the while, her brain kept kicking up more troubling reflections from the ultrasound session.

She'd be relinquishing not one baby but three. What if she was never able to have more? She'd used up a lot of eggs this cycle, and who could tell what the future might bring? But she couldn't keep three children. They needed a real home.

And was it possible Andrew really had misunderstood her desire for children? Or had Stacy driven him away with her eagerness to become a mother? He was the one who'd insisted that they save a lot of money first. Perhaps he'd felt overwhelmed by the responsibilities of fatherhood.

If so, why hadn't he told her?

Pushing her shopping cart distractedly, Stacy smacked into a shelf. She stopped to regain control and replace a couple of cans. There was a question she'd never dared to ask Andrew, and it forced its way to her attention now.

Zora was his high-school sweetheart. What if he

never really loved me? What if she was his true love all along?

That still didn't account for him lying to Zora. And if he never loved Stacy, why had their romance felt so passionate and earnest?

It would explain why he apparently hadn't wanted to have children with her, however. And that hurt.

By the time she returned to the apartment with her arms full of groceries, Stacy had made two decisions. First, since it was impossible to arrive at any conclusions about Andrew, she had to put him out of her mind. Second, on Monday she'd ask the hospital attorney to refer her to an adoption agency. Once she chose a couple, surely this whole situation with triplets would become less troubling.

Feeling some relief that she'd formulated a plan to lay her demons to rest, Stacy set to work preparing for the party.

ON SATURDAY MORNING, Cole took a break in the doctors' lounge between surgeries. The sight of Zack Sargent pouring himself a cup of coffee reminded Cole that here was an excellent potential source of information.

He'd heard a fascinating tale of how Zack got together with his wife. He and Jan had been engaged many years earlier, when she'd become pregnant. Despite some discussion about adoption, Jan had kept their daughter, Kimmie—now school age—after they broke up. Before they met again and reconciled, Zack had been married and widowed, and had a stepdaughter they were also raising. The situation seemed romantic to Cole, so perhaps the obstetrician could offer some pointers.

"May I ask you a question?" Cole asked.

"As long as you promise not to call me Jack."

"I won't." Cole had mixed up the man's name several times. "I wondered how you persuaded Jan not to give up your daughter for adoption."

Zack cast him a dubious look. "Are you serious?"

"I am."

The obstetrician studied him a moment longer, as if to make sure Cole was truly on the level. "I didn't."

"What do you mean?"

"She told me she planned to relinquish Kimmie, and I signed the papers." Zack took a seat on one of the couches. "Six years later, when she accepted the job here, I found out she'd changed her mind and never informed me. Imagine my surprise to learn she was raising our little girl."

Cole tried, and failed, to imagine the situation. "You must have been thrilled," he said.

"Thrilled?" The other doctor studied him in astonishment. "I was furious. I'd missed all those years with Kimmie."

"Then why did you two get married?" Cole persisted. "Was it for your daughter's sake?"

"Why do you ask?"

"I'm trying to figure out some complicated issues in my life," Cole admitted.

"Okay." Zack's head dipped in acknowledgment. "I got over being angry and realized I still loved Jan. We had quite a few issues to work out, though."

"Oh?"

"Just when I assumed we were finally on the same wavelength, she pushed me away." The words came out with a touch of irritation. "She decided I was too controlling."

"How did you win her back?" Cole waited tensely, hoping for a blinding insight.

"I stopped pushing." Zack shrugged. "I discovered I had to let her come to me on her own terms."

"I see." But he didn't. If he let Stacy go, Cole might never see her again, outside work. "Well, thanks."

"You're welcome." The other doctor seemed glad to be done with the conversation. "By the way, I recommend a Christmas wedding. Ours was beautiful."

"I'll keep that in mind."

If Stacy said yes, she could have any type of wedding she wanted, Cole reflected. Of course, if she waited too long, they'd have to wheel her down the aisle with her feet propped up.

That would be just fine with him.

PULLING THE ROUND CAKE LAYERS from the oven, Stacy couldn't believe how much work she still had left to do, with only an hour before the party started. By now, the cakes should be sliced in half horizontally and layered with filling, the chocolate topping melted…and what about the three dozen eggs waiting to be shelled, halved and deviled?

Dropping onto a chair, she called Harper. "I'm running late."

"Are you okay?" her friend responded.

"I hate letting you down. I'm such a screwup."

"Stacy, you're the most reliable person I know. If you don't feel well, I'll understand."

"Nothing's wrong." She hated to admit she'd fallen asleep while the cakes were baking. "How's everything there?"

"Chaotic but fun," her friend responded. "Can you believe a neighbor offered us a kitten this morning? I was planning to wait, but you know how badly Mia wanted one."

"She must be overjoyed."

"Yes, and there's more good news. It looks like I might be accepted as an egg donor!" Harper exclaimed. "I passed the first evaluation and my physical exam went great. I wonder what kind of family will pick me."

Her excitement reminded Stacy of her own, earlier in the process. She wished she was free to enjoy Una's pregnancy and give her support, as she'd planned. Instead, Stacy felt waterlogged and dull-witted. The hard-boiled eggs filling a large pot seemed to mock her. She could almost hear them snickering inside their shells.

I must be losing it.

"I better get to work," she said.

"Oh—the ultrasound!" Harper broke in. "How'd it go?"

Stacy told her.

"Triplets! But you…you haven't changed your mind about…" Her friend's voice trailed off.

"Giving them up? That's still the plan." She braced for an argument.

Instead, Harper said, "I hate when people question my decision to become an egg donor, so if this is the right thing for you, then hooray."

"Thanks." The encouragement felt good.

"Oh, there's Adrienne and Reggie at the door," Harper said.

"Go let them in."

"Mia just did."

"Well, go start the party. I'll be there as soon as I can."

After clicking off, Stacy began to peel the eggs. Although Adrienne had requested that she save the shells for a compost heap, she dumped them in the trash. She couldn't deal with even one more detail.

Before long, shelled and rinsed eggs covered the counter. Another dozen to go, and then there were the cakes to finish.

Stacy stared in dismay. It was ridiculous to get upset about such a small thing, but she felt overwhelmed.

When she heard the front door open, she kept her back toward Cole. Women's emotions made men uncomfortable. Weeping and wailing, as her father called it, had always irritated him, and Andrew's response to any moodiness had been to withdraw.

A tear trailed down her cheek.

Cole came into the kitchen. "Can I help?" The smell of antiseptic was especially strong today.

He'd been assigned a scrub nurse named Anya Meeks, Stacy recalled. Young, pretty, lighthearted.

Everything I used to be.

She cleared her throat. "I'll be done in a minute."

"Doesn't the party start at three?" Cole stood there, taking in the piles of food.

"I'm almost finished," Stacy said.

"No, you aren't." From behind, his arms closed around her. "You're upset."

"Hormones," she muttered thickly.

"Tell me what to do."

No anger. No impatience. Just a matter-of-fact offer to help. It was exactly what Stacy needed. "Okay."

He'd never peeled eggs before, she learned, but the task posed little problem for a surgeon's hands. The same was true of the delicate task of slicing the round cakes into two layers each.

Within half an hour, the eggs had been deviled and the cakes assembled with their filling and chocolate sauce. Stacy didn't mind wiping away the flecks of yellow yolk all over the counter—Cole had been a bit overeager with the beaters—while he filled the dishwasher.

"I have to change clothes." She draped her arms around him. "Thank you."

"My pleasure," Cole murmured.

She lingered, relishing his solid strength and enjoying the way he kissed her hair and massaged her shoulder blades. She felt a stirring deep inside, a longing to be part of him.

"You're a lifesaver." She drew away reluctantly. "I'm not sure why I fell apart."

"My specialty is stitching people together," Cole responded, studying her. He always seemed to be looking for clues to something.

"Back in a minute." Stacy went to put on a clean top and pants. When she returned, it was a little past three. Her spirits lifted at the sight of Cole's finishing touches: he'd packed the Boston cream pies neatly in cake carriers and aligned the deviled eggs inside plastic boxes.

The two of them functioned very well as a team. Not surprising, given that they did that almost daily in the O.R.

They'd planned to drive separately, but why bother? "Let's take my car. It's bigger," Stacy said.

"Good idea." His eyes were dancing.

As for how fellow staffers might react to the sight of them as a couple, she no longer cared.

COLE HAD NEVER ENJOYED parties. Usually, he had no idea what to say, and often he offended people by forgetting their names.

However, he'd never before arrived with such a popular companion, nor with an array of enticing food.

People hurried to help Stacy and him carry in the containers, and dived into the deviled eggs as soon as they were transferred onto platters. Mia and another little girl hopped up and down with excitement when they saw the Boston cream pies, and their mothers narrowly prevented them from sticking their fingers into the chocolate sauce.

Harper's ranch-style rental house, set in a neighborhood of similar homes, was rapidly taking on individuality. By the front steps, Adrienne was busy planting flowers in a freshly turned bed. Arriving guests handed her pots of geraniums, miniature roses and blossoming annuals.

"Gardening is my hobby," she explained when Cole wandered out front to admire her handiwork. "I hired someone to prepare the soil, but I love getting my hands into it. Don't get much chance these days, with my schedule."

Having grown up in a condominium, Cole had never taken an interest in gardening. It looked like fun. "What about vegetables? That would be more practical than flowers."

"They tend to look raggedy in a front yard," Adrienne said. "One of these days I'll have you over to my house. It's got a nice big yard with an herb garden, and I always plant a few tomatoes."

More people arrived. While Cole didn't remember all their names, he remembered more than he'd expected. Unlike in Minnesota, where he'd kept his private life and personal ideas separate from work, he chatted with many of these people on a range of topics.

Not everything went smoothly. Ned Norwalk pointedly avoided him, making Cole sorry he'd snapped at the nurse about moving in with Stacy. Not too sorry, though. And he wasn't pleased when a staffer's daughter, Tammy, a journalism student at California State University, Fullerton, asked if she could interview Dr. Daddy Crisis for her blog.

"I'd rather let that nonsense die a quiet death," Cole told her.

At Tammy's disappointed look, her mother, nurse Eva Rogers, gave her a poke. "I warned you," she said sternly.

Tammy scrunched her face. "What kind of reporter would I be if I didn't try?"

Cole hurried away. Yet, despite feeling a bit awkward, he didn't try to stick to Stacy's side. These were her friends and she seemed to enjoy circulating freely.

No one mentioned the triplets. As far as he could tell, Stacy wasn't spreading the news about that yet. He was glad, especially with Miss Would-Be Journalist hanging about.

Standing alone with a glass of punch in hand, Cole noted the way people cast him speculative glances. Wondering about his relationship with Stacy? Well, so was he.

On the rear patio, a handful of guests clustered around a snack table set up with the deviled eggs, as well as chips and dips and a cheese tray. Having eaten more than his share of the eggs while fixing them, Cole wasn't tempted to join in.

He found a deck chair near Adrienne, who'd finished her gardening duties and stretched out on a lounger for some well-deserved rest. "I'm amazed at the lack of flies in California," he told her. "All this food and nothing buzzing around."

"I take it for granted, probably because I grew up here." The doctor had brushed out the long blond hair she usually wore in a twist. She was an attractive woman, Cole realized, although her loose sweater and casual jeans indicated she didn't fuss about appearances.

He sat beside her, watching a group of children play catch on the grass. Mia stayed on the sidelines, cradling a kitten and cheering on her friends. "Good throw, Reggie!" she called to a blond boy, who flashed her a grin minus a couple of teeth.

"That's my nephew." Adrienne sighed. "He's growing fast."

Stacy had mentioned that Adrienne was raising the boy after her sister's death in a car crash a few months ago. "It must be hard, adjusting to parenthood," Cole said.

"I've had plenty of practice." The obstetrician stretched her shoulders. "After our mother died three years ago, I took this job at Safe Harbor partly so I could help with Reggie. My sister was bipolar and abused alcohol, like both our parents. Reggie needed stability in his life, and I'm it."

Although surprised by her frankness about such personal matters, Cole appreciated the confidence. "Your long hours must make it hard to spend time with him."

"It's far from ideal, but I do the best I can." She closed her eyes, and he recalled that she must have been on duty overnight. A moment later, she opened them to glance toward her nephew.

Keeping watch. Must be her maternal instincts.

"You love him a lot," Cole observed.

She sat up straighter. "Reggie's a great little guy, a real trooper. I just wish I didn't have to leave him with sitters so often."

"You're adopting him?" Cole asked. "I presume that's necessary, even with a family relationship."

"I want him to feel secure that I'll always be there," Adrienne noted. "It's basically a formality. Vicki's will appointed me guardian. Reggie's father was one of those hit-and-run jobs."

Ouch. Cole wondered if that was a dig at him.

Adrienne smiled. "Stop scowling. I didn't mean you."

"You sure?"

"You're obviously pitching in," she said.

"Doing my best." He couldn't resist asking. "Do you think Stacy's going to regret giving up the triplets for adoption?"

Adrienne raised her hand in a warning. Realizing he'd lost track of who was nearby, Cole scanned the area. Eva's daughter stood not far off, idly observing the children. Or so it appeared.

"Do you think she heard?"

Adrienne gave a headshake, as if to caution him. She must also suspect the young woman of eavesdropping.

Cole remembered his mother granting interviews to science and medical reporters, who'd always respected her boundaries. He decided to hope for the best. Tammy was Eva's daughter, after all.

Besides, here came Mia with a squirming black-and-white kitten in her arms. "Hi, Dr. Rattigan. This is Po."

"How'd you pick the name?"

"Like *Kung Fu Panda,*" she said. "He's black-and-white, too."

"He's cute." Cole reached out to pat the soft fur.

Through the rear sliding door, Harper announced, "The caterer's here! Come eat dinner while it's hot."

Cole checked his watch. "It's only four-thirty."

"Does eating early break some universal law?" Adrienne teased.

"I guess I should go with the flow, huh?"

His companion patted his arm. "I'm starting to like you." Then she called, "Wash your hands, Reggie!" and vanished into the interior, along with a rush of children.

Cole followed in their wake, not sure how to take Adrienne's comment, and concluding that he might as well consider it a compliment.

Chapter Fifteen

Despite her intention of seeking a referral, Stacy kept putting off contacting the hospital attorney. The party had left her with a warm glow, and many images of children and their parents playing and joking and sharing a meal. Little Mia with the kitten sleeping in her lap. Reggie managing to smear goop on his face within minutes after washing. Zack's daughters, Berry and Kimmie, singing "There's No Place Like Home" as a sort of blessing over the food.

Several times Stacy got as far as pressing the elevator button for the fifth floor, where Tony had his office. But once she brought in other people, the babies wouldn't be hers anymore. Considering how strongly she'd reacted to the news that Una was carrying her babies, how much worse would she feel about losing the little ones nestled inside her own body?

Common sense told Stacy to see a counselor. Yet even though Laird had muttered an apology for his drunken behavior at the club, she certainly couldn't talk to him. Consulting a counselor outside the staff would be expensive. And pointless. Because ultimately, this was her decision. And she'd made it.

Stacy drew up a list of desirable characteristics for

adoptive parents. Married for at least three years. Financially stable. Preferably home owners. Although she didn't want an open adoption, she'd like for them to send her annual letters.

Yet when she tried to imagine her children with their adoptive—no, make that *real*—family, other scenarios kept sneaking in. Cole holding babies on his lap. Cole setting dinner on a table surrounded by children. Cole lining up three kids before school, inspecting their clothes and lunches.

He'd be a good father and he wanted to marry her, but just because it was Stacy's nature to make others happy didn't mean she should take the easy way out. Not that raising triplets would be easy, exactly, but it might seem that way at the start. Then, in a year or so, she'd wake up with a houseful of stubborn, messy toddlers, a politely distant husband and the realization that she'd never find the love she craved.

What she needed was a pep talk from her mom. Stacy had intended to call her, anyway, to tell her about the triplets. But did they have to continue keeping the pregnancy secret from her dad? Alastair might be a reserved and occasionally stern father, but he loved her.

So when her phone sounded as she was finishing dinner on Thursday, Stacy felt a rush of pleasure at seeing her father's name on the screen. Mom must have broken down and told him. Even though the conversation might be prickly at first, she craved his reassurance.

"Dad!" she said.

His response curdled the food in her stomach and filled her with disbelief.

ON THURSDAYS, Cole didn't perform surgery. Instead, he spent the mornings on administrative tasks. That involved coordinating with a team of reproductive endocrinologists, nurses and technicians, reviewing proposals for studies, overseeing applications for grants and tracking fertility success rates. He also served on the boards of several national fertility organizations and had to keep up with their activities.

After lunch he saw patients and performed office procedures. By late afternoon, he began to sense a stir around him—phones ringing more than usual and staff members murmuring to each other—but he refused to allow curiosity to interfere with his focus on patient care. At work, Cole left his cell phone on vibrate, even though he rarely felt the damn thing. If anything required his immediate attention, his nurse, Lucky, would inform him.

Thanks to a couple of cancellations, he finished earlier than expected, at around six-thirty. After inputting his notes on the last patient, Cole ran into Eva, who was hovering nervously outside his office. Lucky stood nearby glowering at her.

"Is something wrong?" he asked, unsure which of them to address.

"I want to apologize." Eva sounded breathless.

"For what?"

"Have you looked out the window lately?" she asked.

He hadn't. When he moved onto the fourth floor, Cole had been disappointed to discover he had a boring northern view that included the parking area and adjacent street, rather than the ocean to the south. Owen had explained apologetically that this was the only available suite large enough to accommodate Cole's practice.

"Don't let them see you," Lucky warned, as Cole reached for the rod to adjust his blinds.

That didn't sound good.

Below, in the lingering June sunlight, a crowd milled between TV vans and portable spotlights. While a few members of the press had staked out the hospital's entrance, most faced the office building, no doubt aware that he was in there.

"What the hell?" Cole said.

"I'll show you." At the computer, Lucky brought up a live image of the same scene from ground level. A reporter Cole recognized from the day of his speech faced the camera, talking excitedly.

"We're waiting to chat with Dr. Cole Rattigan, aka Dr. Daddy Crisis," the man intoned. "A journalism student's report that's gone viral on the internet contends that the doctor has impregnated his nurse with triplets. Famous for predicting that birthrates will plummet due to degenerated sperm, Dr. Rattigan appears to have no trouble with his own reproductive prowess."

Cole suddenly wished he'd developed a more colorful vocabulary of swear words. He'd never felt the need for them, until now.

"I'm sorry." Concern laced Eva's voice. "I had no idea she'd pull this."

Cole took out his phone. It showed text and voice messages from Jennifer and Owen. Nothing from Stacy. Had she heard about this?

He was glad he hadn't given his old landlady the new address, preferring to forward his mail via the post office.

"Now what?" he asked aloud. Experience taught that confronting reporters would only make matters worse. They'd twist his words, and might even follow him home.

"I'll get rid of them," Lucky announced.

Cole regarded his nurse dubiously. Prior to attending nursing school, Lucky had driven an ambulance and worked as a paramedic. He'd also been a bouncer in a bar, drawing on his background growing up in a rough part of L.A. "I don't want you to get in trouble."

"No trouble." Lucky flashed a confident grin. "This should be fun."

Eva's eyes widened. "Are you sure?"

"Trust me." Adjusting the bar pin that proclaimed him Luke Mendez, R.N., he added, "Keep watching that screen." And out he went.

Eva clasped her hands in front of her. "Tammy had no right to post personal medical information about Stacy. She could get me fired. I swear, I didn't mention anything in front of her."

"This is my fault," Cole conceded. "I was talking to Adrienne at the party and it didn't occur to me that anyone might be listening."

"She shouldn't have repeated a private conversation." Eva shook her head angrily. "My husband and I raised our kids to have more integrity than that. Our son's in the air force. He would never pull a stunt like this for his own advancement. I didn't think Tammy would, either."

On the screen, the reporter was informing any new viewers that Dr. Daddy Crisis was about to become the unmarried father of triplets. At the lobby entrance, patients and staff members blinked in surprise as they emerged, some stopping to ask questions, others ducking past the crowd.

He ought to call Jennifer or Owen, Cole reflected.

He'd jumped the gun by authorizing his nurse to intervene.

Too late now. The lobby doors disgorged a familiar muscular fellow in a navy nurse's uniform. Lucky had rolled up his sleeves to reveal his tattoos, which included a colorful dragon on one side and a sexy cartoon woman wearing skimpy armor and wielding a sword on the other. Raising his arms, he gestured the throng to silence.

"Who're you?" demanded a reporter, thrusting out his microphone. Others followed suit.

"My name is Luke Mendez, R.N.," he replied in a voice loud enough to carry to the far reaches of the parking lot. "I'm Dr. Cole Rattigan's nurse, and I can assure you that I am *not* pregnant."

A stunned silence was broken moments later by a scattering of embarrassed questions. It didn't seem to occur to anyone that Cole also had a scrub nurse. No doubt they'd figure it out soon enough, but for now, the announcement had knocked the wind out of everyone's sails.

The newscast cut to an anchorwoman at a desk, who hurriedly changed the subject. "In Sacramento today, the state legislature failed once again to agree on a balanced budget despite the approaching deadline…."

Cole closed the internet site. "That was brilliant."

"It won't last," Eva said, "but maybe they'll be more cautious next time. I hope Tammy's ashamed. She should to be."

"Any idea what Lucky's drinking these days?" Cole asked. "I'll send him a case."

"Fruit juice," Eva said. "I've seen him shopping at the health food store."

"Good to know." Cole decided to buy him a gift certificate.

This wasn't over, not by a long shot. But he appreciated the breather.

A short while later, having thanked Lucky, spoken to Jennifer and Owen and ordered the gift certificate, Cole ventured into the now-empty lot and cycled home. How wonderful to travel undisturbed, filling his lungs with the sea breeze.

At the apartment, he found Stacy's dinner dishes still on the table. He went in search of her.

She lay on her bed, her face blotchy with tears. Although he'd seen her cry before, Cole had never witnessed this look of utter devastation.

"I'm so sorry." Gingerly, he sat on the edge of her bed. "Tammy heard me talking to Adrienne at the party. I had no idea she'd broadcast our personal news."

"My father called." The misery in her eyes tore at his heart. "He's disgusted with me. He's angry with my mom, too, because he figures I must have told her I was pregnant. I did, although not about the triplets."

"He'll get over it." Cole might have little experience with fathers, but he knew how *he'd* react if this happened in his family.

Stacy's mouth quivered. "He said I've humiliated him and the whole family. My sister won't be able to hold her head up in church because of me."

"It can't be much of a church if they blame her for her sister's actions." Cole's logical response didn't seem to make a dent in Stacy's unhappiness, though.

"He says the only way he'll forgive me is if I get married," Stacy went on.

"That's wrong," Cole blurted. "Love shouldn't be conditional."

"Is this what you wanted? To pressure me into marrying you? Is this why you mentioned the triplets in front of Tammy?"

"Of course not!" Surely she didn't believe that. But Cole was beginning to learn that, with Stacy, emotions sometimes overrode reason.

She folded her arms, anger yielding to steely determination. "You have to leave."

"Okay." Best to wait till she was calmer. "We can talk tomorrow."

Stacy shook her head. "I mean leave the apartment."

He stared at her. After all they'd been through, she was throwing him out when she needed him most?

"It's not safe for you to be alone." Her pregnancy grew more complicated by the day, as the triplets put extra demands on her body. "Please think this over."

"And wait until the press finds out we're living together?" Stacy demanded. "Oh, that'll be lovely! Dr. Daddy Crisis cohabiting with his trashy, pregnant nurse."

"You are not trashy," Cole said.

"My father thinks I am."

If these were the old days, Cole would have challenged her father to a duel. Mr. Layne had no business hurting Stacy this way. "Let me take care of you."

"Pack your stuff and move out," she answered, ignoring the tears coursing down her cheeks. "Now!"

He bit back the arguments that sprang to mind. She did have a point about the press. If it meant this much to her, he'd go.

For now.

ON FRIDAY MORNING at the hospital, Cole was all business. Not that Stacy expected anything else, but without realizing it, she'd come to relish those sideways glances that spoke louder than words. Instead, he greeted her with a distant nod when he spotted her in the hall, and went to scrub.

When she discovered he had asked another nurse to assist him with gowning, she nearly pushed the woman aside before getting a grip on herself. The discovery that it was Anya—twenty-five-year-old, bubbly Anya, who gazed at him adoringly—only made Stacy angrier.

Cole had moved out last night. She hadn't expected it to happen so fast. With his customary efficiency, he'd rented rooms at Harbor Suites, a motel near the medical center that leased rooms by the week. The place catered to families of patients who didn't want to make a long daily drive.

He'd apologized for leaving his bed and large TV, promising to fetch them when he found an apartment. Since he'd paid half her rent for the entire month, Stacy could hardly object.

She didn't want to object. In fact, she'd sneaked into his room late at night and lain down, just for a minute, to breathe in the reassuring scent clinging to the mattress. And to wish that for once he hadn't been so darned agreeable.

If he really loved me... He'd do what? Disregard her wishes? Dragging herself back to her room, Stacy had wished she could think straight.

By Friday afternoon, she didn't feel any better. Cole had remained coolly polite through two surgeries, and then adjourned to his office without a word.

Mercifully, there were no reporters dogging the hospital grounds. All the same, Stacy could feel her father's outraged disappointment vibrating all the way from Utah.

That only stiffened her resolve. Nobody was going to push her into a foolish marriage. The sooner she settled matters, the better.

After her shift, she called Tony Franco, who agreed to talk to her right away. The attorney was an enthusiastic supporter of the fertility program. He'd met his wife when, as a surrogate, she'd become pregnant with his daughter, now a preschooler.

In the fifth floor administrative suite, a secretary ushered Stacy into his large, book-lined office. Behind the broad desk, a window overlooked the Pacific Ocean a few blocks away.

A calm man with rust-brown hair, Tony sprang up to shake hands. He directed Stacy into an upholstered chair and, after an inquiry about how she was feeling, provided her with a list of adoption agencies and attorneys.

"It's rather early in the pregnancy to make a decision like this," he noted.

Stacy squirmed, feeling achy despite the comfortable chair. "I don't want to put it off."

Tony handed her a legal-looking document. "The father will need to sign this relinquishment paper."

"What?" Stacy bristled.

"He has to agree to the adoption."

"That's not fair!" This was her body and her decision.

Tony regarded her sympathetically. "You're not the first woman to whom this has come as a shock, believe me. If you prefer, I could give this to Cole."

And let someone else, even a well-intentioned man like Tony, meddle in her affairs? "I'll handle this. But thank you." After putting the paper atop the list of agencies, she shook hands again and departed.

Cole was no more responsible for the laws than Tony was, yet having to get his permission rankled. Stacy decided to get this over with tonight.

Chapter Sixteen

Until now, Cole had never cared much about his surroundings. A plain apartment with serviceable furnishings suited him fine. So did a tiny kitchenette with a couple of burners and a microwave. So what if you couldn't bake brownies or a Boston cream pie?

But arriving at his tiny suite shortly before seven, he felt his spirits plummet. In the past few weeks, he'd grown accustomed to Stacy's delicate furniture and to the lingering scents of baking. Mostly, he missed knowing she was there, even if she might be in a grumpy mood. Since she hadn't acted this way before she got pregnant, he blamed her condition. Besides, he enjoyed teasing her into a better frame of mind.

Over a frozen dinner, he put a DVD into his laptop and sat at the chipped table to watch it. Usually, the comedic tension of two people falling in love while denying it amused him. Tonight, he found himself picking apart the movie's shallow concepts.

If he'd learned anything from his clumsy attempts to analyze his colleagues' marriages, it was that lovers also had to be friends. They and their spouses formed partnerships that nurtured each other as well as their children. It added to the fun when people surprised each other with loving gestures and gifts, but day by day, it was the little things that counted. Or was he deluding himself because he didn't seem capable of sweeping Stacy off her feet?

Hearing a knock on the door, Cole paused the movie. Cautiously, he went to the front window. Although the press had backed off, some pushy reporter might have tracked him here.

Against the uninspiring backdrop of the motel courtyard, Stacy's flushed face glowed in the June twilight. Cole banged his shin against a chair in his hurry to open the door.

"Hi," he said, not bothering to conceal his happiness at seeing her.

She held up an official-looking sheet of paper. "I need you to sign this."

It couldn't be divorce papers, since they weren't married. Taking it, Cole moved back. "Come in."

She edged past him, the vivid plum color of her blouse and the scent of lilies instantly making the room more congenial. As she gazed around, her expression softened. "Sorry. I didn't mean to be so abrupt."

"That's okay." He scanned the document. *Relinquish all rights...* "Is this necessary?"

"Yes, according to Tony." Stacy hovered close by.

Cole couldn't bring himself to slash his signature on the bottom, no matter how much she obviously wanted him to. "I never sign legal papers without reviewing them carefully." That was true, if incomplete. "Is there a rush?"

She drew herself up. "I want to get this over with."

"You realize the adoption can't be finalized until after the babies are born, anyway," Cole pointed out. "I'm not saying you'll change your mind..."

"How come everyone else thinks they know better than me how I should lead my life?" she snapped. When she turned away, he saw that her eyes were bright with tears.

Her father's rejection must be haunting her. But this was a life-altering decision. It shouldn't be reached in a burst of emotion.

"Stacy, I'd like for us to see a counselor." Where had that come from? "Not Laird," Cole added quickly.

"No." She hugged herself.

"You're making a choice that will affect your entire life," he pointed out. "Mine, too. Don't you want to be sure we've considered all the angles?"

Her breathing speeded up. As if afraid she might burst, she moved to the still-open door. "If you insist on reading the fine print, that's up to you. Just leave it in my box at the hospital."

Then she was gone. Swallowing the bitterness of regret, Cole forced himself to face the truth.

Even if, through some stratagem, he managed to skirt Stacy's defenses and win her hand, she would never really love him. During the past few months, he'd come to acknowledge his limitations as well as his strengths. He was a straightforward guy, brilliant in his field and with previously unsuspected fatherly instincts, but he would never send Stacy's heartbeat into overdrive by singing to her in front of a crowd. Nor would he astound her by presenting her the perfect gift at the perfect moment.

She had to love him for who he was and despite his flaws, the way he loved her. And that wasn't going to happen.

Outside, kids rattled by on skateboards, calling to each other. On the laptop, a motionless image showed two actors pretending to flirt. If he touched a key, dialogue written by a screenwriter would flow from their mouths. They'd be witty and glib, and if they got hurt, the emotions would bounce right off them. Unlike the ache he felt.

Cole had never imagined falling in love and losing. Love meant too much. In a way, he'd been glad he was always the one who drifted away or, in Felicia's case, acted like a jerk—her opinion, not his. He'd never wanted to vibrate with this hollow, lost sense the way he had on the airplane coming home from France.

He hadn't even realized he was developing these feelings for Stacy. They'd grown undetected, day by day, as the two of them worked together. Then one night, not only had he made love to her almost by accident, he'd also tumbled over the edge between liking and adoring. Needing.

Hurting.

If only she would let him take care of her and the babies during the pregnancy. Cole clenched his fists as if to fight an unseen enemy.

To calm himself, he switched from the DVD to an online newscast. A couple of routine items rolled by, and he'd just risen to fix a bowl of ice cream when he heard his name.

Dourly, he turned toward the screen. There, against a backdrop of trees, walkways and tall buildings—almost certainly a college campus—a young woman with thick glasses and wispy hair stood perspiring as she faced a knot of reporters.

Eva's daughter was getting a taste of what she'd unleashed. All the same, Cole felt sorry for her.

"Everything I know, I put in my blog," Tammy was saying.

"Who did Dr. Rattigan impregnate, Miss Rogers?" a woman demanded. "Or did you invent the whole story?"

"I did not!"

"It clearly wasn't his nurse," said a man.

Behind them, a group of students gathered to watch. They reminded Cole of observers at a car wreck.

"He has more than one nurse!" Tammy exclaimed. "Oh, who cares?"

"What's her name?" the woman demanded.

Don't you dare tell them. Cole held his breath.

"You people must be short on real news, or maybe you don't know what real news is."

"Do you?" someone asked. Then Cole realized he'd spoken aloud in the empty room.

Clearly on the verge of a meltdown, Tammy wavered. Any second, she might reveal Stacy's name and transform a difficult situation into a disaster.

Then her back stiffened. "It's none of your business," she said. "And thanks to you guys, I'm changing my major. Maybe I'll be a nurse like my mom. I sure don't want to be like you—a pack of wolves. No, not wolves. Jackals."

That stopped them long enough for Tammy to flee. Cole would have been tempted to send her a thank-you bouquet, except that she'd started this whole mess.

Her words didn't seem to register. At least, not with the woman who spoke directly into the camera. "So Dr. Daddy Crisis has more than one nurse. Is it like a harem? We'll get to the bottom of this. Reporting from Cal State Fullerton, this is..."

Cole had to defend Stacy. Even though he no longer deluded himself that he could devise a tactic to win her heart, he had to stop the gossipmongers in their tracks.

Fortunately, there were responsible reporters in the world. Not everyone lived from scandal to scandal.

And he had an idea how to enlist one of them.

ON SATURDAY MORNING, Stacy awoke to an eerie silence. It wasn't really all that silent, since she could hear traffic from the street and music pouring from someone's window. But in the apartment, she was alone.

Although Cole hadn't yet removed his furniture, something vital was missing. She lay in bed wondering if Anya was assisting him in surgery this morning. Perhaps meaning to be kind, the nursing coordinator had promised Stacy no more Saturday shifts for the duration of her pregnancy. She wished Betsy wasn't such a nice boss.

Finally Stacy dragged herself out of bed, showered and ate. She should take a walk, or go shopping. Maybe visit a museum.

Was Cole home yet? If she stopped by his place, she was afraid he'd think she was pressuring him about signing the paper. Back when he'd loomed as an intimidating, famous surgeon and she was simply his scrub nurse, she used to bake cookies or cupcakes to bring to work just to inspire a rare smile from him. She'd like to bring back that smile now.

What was wrong with her?

When the phone rang, she snatched it eagerly from the table. But the screen showed Harper's name. "What's up?"

"It's Una," Harper said. "She asked me to call you. She suffered a fall."

"Is she okay?" Stacy felt guilty for wallowing in her own misery. Una might be seriously injured.

"Just bruised, but she's afraid of miscarrying," her

friend responded. "Her husband's here and we're arranging an ultrasound at the office. She'd like your support."

"I'll be right there." It occurred to Stacy that Harper didn't normally work on Saturdays. "Dr. Franco asked you to come in on your day off? Who's watching Mia?"

"I took her to Adrienne's," her friend said. "She and Reggie are planting a vegetable garden."

"Sounds like fun." Stacy's thoughts returned to Una. *Please let her be okay.* "I'll be there as fast as I can."

"See you." Harper clicked off.

If Una lost the twins… Stacy refused to dwell on that idea.

Positive thoughts only.

A minute later, she was en route.

"I'M STILL NOT CONVINCED this is a good idea," Jennifer Martin said as Cole took a seat behind the conference table. "But Dr. Rayburn gave the okay."

Her husband, a blond man with an intense manner, angled one of the lights. The videographer, a young bearded fellow named Paul Gupta, studied the effect from behind his videocam. "That's perfect. No shadows."

Stepping away, Ian Martin assessed Cole with a glance. "Shift your chair a little to the left. Excellent."

How strange to be deliberately subjecting himself to more publicity, Cole mused. "I appreciate your concern, Jennifer. But they're not going to quit hounding me and I can't let them go after Stacy."

"Just doing their jobs, in an obnoxious way." Ian had worked for an international news agency before meeting Jennifer and moving to Safe Harbor. "I'm glad to be out of that rat race." He wrote nonfiction books on medical topics now, in addition to producing a weekly online news program.

The public relations director, wearing a blouse and dress pants instead of her usual suit, began to pace. After receiving Cole's call last night, she'd moved swiftly. She'd secured the administrator's approval, cleared it with her husband and arranged for them to use this conference room at the hospital.

Everyone involved was trustworthy, she'd assured Cole. The shooting and editing would be fair and professional. Even the videographer belonged to the Safe Harbor Medical family. Paul's mother, Devina, was the office nurse for pediatrician Samantha Forrest. While his older brother had gone to medical school, he was pursuing his dream of becoming a filmmaker.

"I'd be more comfortable if you'd tell me exactly what you plan to say," Jennifer fretted.

"This isn't a scripted show." Ian took his place beside Cole at the table.

"You have notes," she pointed out.

Her husband glanced at his cards. "Questions, not answers."

"If I say something stupid, you can edit it out, right?" Cole said.

"Sure, but we may disagree on what's stupid," Ian replied.

Hold on. Seized by a fierce desire to ride into battle, Cole had plunged into the fray, assuming that being interviewed by the PR director's husband was safe. He hadn't prepared an outline, although he did have general ideas.

He planned to put the issues into perspective for the public, to counteract the exaggerations in the press.

Maybe then everyone would leave him and his nurse alone. "You won't use Stacy's name."

"I already promised not to," Ian confirmed.

"Maybe I should concentrate on sperm rates and how the future of mankind is not on the chopping block," Cole fretted. "After all, I'm a scientist."

"I thought you wanted to scoop the media," Ian answered coolly. "You can't do that unless people watch this."

"Which means, uh, what?" Cole asked.

Jennifer was pacing across the room. "It means you have to give them human interest stuff."

"Such as getting she-who-shall-not-be-named pregnant," Ian clarified. "The personal angle."

No wonder Jennifer wished he'd written a script. No wonder she had reservations about the whole idea.

Nevertheless, Cole refused to back down. He'd accepted that he and Stacy had no future together. It didn't matter if he made himself look foolish, as long as he kept her safe.

"Ready?" Paul asked.

Cole took a deep breath.

"This won't hurt," Ian assured him. "Much. Okay, let's do it."

It was too late to change his mind.

Chapter Seventeen

When she'd missed Una's first ultrasound, Stacy had never imagined they'd be back for a repeat so soon. She only wished the circumstances were better.

Zora was setting up the ultrasound equipment when Harper ushered Stacy into the examining room. On the table, Una lay biting her lip, while James held her hand. Dr. Franco, who'd thrown a white coat over her jeans and T-shirt, observed from beside the counter.

Stacy paused near the entrance. "What happened?"

"You're here!" Una reached toward her, and James tactfully stepped aside. But why was this woman reaching for Stacy instead of her husband?

"Harper called." Stacy drew closer, and felt Una's hand close over hers.

"I can't believe I was so careless!" Una flinched as Zora applied gel to her bare stomach, which was visibly enlarged already, at nine weeks. "I was in the backyard when the phone rang inside. I slipped on the back steps and my tummy hit the concrete."

Stacy could see a purpling bruise near Una's exposed hip. "Did you suffer any internal bleeding?"

"No," Una said. "But…Stacy, promise me something." Her grip tightened.

Although tempted to agree regardless of what the favor might be, Stacy merely asked, "What can I do?"

"Promise that if I lose the twins, you'll let me adopt the triplets," she begged. "You're giving them up anyway, right?"

It was a reasonable request. Her friend's previous demand would have left the Barkers raising five babies and a toddler, which wasn't fair to the children. But if the twins were gone…

"You aren't going to miscarry," Stacy said. "If the mother isn't seriously injured in a fall, it's rare for it to harm the baby."

"And we're about to find out," Dr. Franco interjected. "Look."

On screen, moving shadows formed into two distinct shapes. The hearts were beating and the little creatures wiggling.

"Oh, thank God!" Una breathed. "I can see a tiny leg. Are those toes?"

"I doubt you can make them out yet, but they are formed," Dr. Franco told her.

Zora kept her head down, concentrating on her work. Even at an angle, it was obvious the technician had red-rimmed eyes. She must have partied too hard last night. Stacy pictured Andrew tossing back beers at a party, one arm encircling Zora's waist, teeth gleaming as he laughed.

Something was missing from her mental movie. It took a moment for her to figure out what.

No pain.

Stacy didn't care that he'd been with Zora and not her. Whatever grip Andrew had retained on her emotions had vanished, like an old injury that had unexpectedly healed.

"You're right—they're fine." Una beamed at the doctor. "Can we tell the sex yet?"

"It's a bit early," Zora replied. "Are you in a hurry?"

Una and James shook their heads at almost the same instant. "We're just glad they're okay," he said, reclaiming his wife's hand.

No one commented on the fact that Stacy hadn't agreed to let them adopt the triplets. As things had turned out, it didn't matter. But why hadn't she said yes?

With a congratulatory farewell, Stacy retreated. Harper and the obstetrician remained, but after negotiating her cart through the cramped space, Zora exited behind her. Politely, Stacy held the door.

At close range, Zora didn't look hungover. She'd been crying.

"Are you okay?" For nearly three years, Stacy had harbored resentment toward this woman. Today, she felt only concern.

Zora pushed the cart jerkily along the hall. "I could tell how much you love the triplets."

The comment startled Stacy, but she had no time to reflect on it. "Is this about babies?"

"In a sense." She took a deep breath. "You were right. Andrew lied to me. About you not wanting kids and about a lot of things. He isn't the man I thought he was."

"You knew he was cheating on me when you took up with him," Stacy pointed out.

"I told myself he'd been mine all along." Zora opened the door to a storage room. "In high school, when he dumped me, I couldn't believe it was over. So when I ran into him again and he said I'd always been his true love, I fell for it."

He said I was the love of his life. Stacy braced instinctively for the familiar twist of pain, but it was gone. She felt only regret for wasted years and broken trust. "Now what will you do?"

"I left him." Zora angled the sonogram equipment into a space. "After finding out he lied, I started snooping through his email and discovered he's been fooling around when he travels. He tried to deny it, but after a while he shrugged and said that's the way guys are. That I shouldn't make a big deal of it."

A memory surfaced. Stacy had caught a whiff of unfamiliar perfume on Andrew's clothes when he'd returned from a business trip. Afraid of overreacting, she'd called her mother, who'd advised her to trust him. Nothing drove a man away faster than suspicion and nagging, Ellen had said. Stacy had followed her advice, but he'd dropped her, anyway. Most likely he'd been cheating all along.

"You're lucky to have a straight shooter like Dr. Rattigan," Zora added.

"I don't have—" Stacy broke off when she saw people leaving the examining room. Just as well. Because she didn't care to finish that sentence.

She no longer knew whether she had him or not. Or what any of this meant, except that some of her biggest assumptions had been wrong.

"I APPRECIATE THE HELP," Adrienne Cavill said on Sunday as Cole, dressed in his oldest jeans and a worn shirt, turned a shovelful of soil in a corner of her garden. "I got so inspired working at Harper's house, I went overboard."

Feeling confined in his rooms, and tired of searching for rentals on the internet, Cole had called the obstetrician. He'd only meant to accept her offer of showing him her garden, but when he learned she was embarked on a major vegetable-planting project, he'd volunteered to help.

The two-story Craftsman-style house in the northern part of Safe Harbor had a large rear yard. There was space for a garden, lawn, covered patio and several pathways with hard surfaces for Reggie's tricycle. The little boy alternately zoomed around and raced across the lawn to climb on the play equipment.

"Does he ever run out of energy?" Cole asked.

A grin creased Adrienne's dirt-smeared face. "He operates at full speed until he collapses." She resumed spreading compost. "He and Mia worked hard yesterday."

"The kids enjoy gardening?" Cole stretched his back.

Adrienne pointed to another area. "We planted seeds over there. Of course, I spent almost as much time cleaning them up afterward."

"You hosed them down?" That must have been a cute scene.

"I rinsed off the worst of it," she said. "Then we went inside. You wouldn't believe the dirt rings I scrubbed out of the tub."

"I like dirt." Cole studied the rich loam. He was enjoying this more than he'd expected. "So this section is for tomatoes?" A half-dozen nursery plants on the patio table awaited planting.

"My favorite varieties. Mostly heirlooms." Adrienne swiped at her cheek with a sleeve, banishing a gnat and leaving a dark streak. "When I was growing up, we used to make spaghetti sauce from scratch. I don't have time anymore, so I've collected plenty of quickie pasta recipes. Just chop the tomatoes and stick them in the microwave."

"I'd like a garden someday." Cole had never imagined such a thing until recently. "Along with a couple of kids to hose off. How about you?"

"Reggie's it for me," Adrienne said. "Medical reasons." Without elaborating, she went to fetch more compost.

On the walkway, the little boy whizzed by. "I'm flying!" He held up his hands for an instant before grabbing the handlebars, narrowly averting a spill.

Yearning squeezed Cole so hard he could barely hang on to the shovel. Yearning for a garden like this. For children. Above all, for the right woman to share them with.

He believed he'd found her, but Stacy had sent him away. Still, his need for a home and family kept growing stronger.

Cole didn't see how he could move on when he loved her so much. But maybe he had to.

ANDREW WAS A CHEATER and a liar. He hadn't simply been overcome by love for another woman. Instead, he'd cheated on Zora, too.

Sitting on the carpet in her living room, Stacy spent Sunday afternoon doing something utterly childish. She'd brought some of her favorite toys out from her storage unit, planning to give them to Una. Now she set up a marble run, a series of curved plastic pieces with towers and spirals. Then she released her beloved old glass marbles one by one at the top, watching in weird fascination as they swooped around and over and down, landing with a clink in a receptacle.

A plastic piece shifted slightly and one of the marbles got stuck. *Chunk!* A second marble ran into the blockage. *Chunk!* Soon there were half a dozen marbles lodged in a row, waiting for Stacy to free them.

The blockage resembled her life these past few years. She'd been stuck behind the roadblock of her marriage, unable to move past the question of how such a deep and abiding love could vanish. Was it her schedule combined with Andrew's travel? Was there some flaw in her?

All the while, Stacy could see, she'd been jiggling the wrong part of the marble run. The problem hadn't been her, or their schedules. It had been Andrew. Beautiful, self-assured, narcissistic Andrew.

How could she have been so blind? The fact that he'd fooled Zora as well did nothing to assuage the embarrassment at her own gullibility.

Reaching down, Stacy straightened the piece, and the marbles resumed their roller-coaster journey through the plastic channels. But she wasn't fixed. Not yet.

Leaning against the foot of the couch, Stacy mentally retraced her actions and reactions nearly three years ago, when Andrew had dumped her.

Naturally, she'd turned to her friends. Harper, having just lost her husband, had sympathized, but couldn't provide much insight. Vicki, who periodically went off her medications, had been careening through the hyperactive phase of her bipolar disorder and was in no condition to advise anyone. Although Adrienne had moved in with her sister to help out, Stacy hadn't known her very well. Besides, Adrienne had never been married.

So she'd called her mother. Ellen had come through with loving support, and so had Dad, in his low-key way. Devastated and clinging to their love, Stacy had never asked the questions that troubled her now.

Why did you tell me not to trust my instincts about Andrew's cheating? Did you truly believe that burying my head in the sand would save my marriage?

Scooping up the marbles, she dropped them again into the top tray. Unobstructed, they sped downward, scooting along bridges and accelerating as the angle grew steeper. But despite having a clearer view of marriage, Stacy still felt blocked.

Why couldn't I see Andrew for who he really was? Was I instinctively playing peacemaker, the way I'd always done with my parents? Was this partly my fault, after all?

Stacy was suffering, not over Andrew but over her father's rejection. She'd expected him to take her side in whatever choice she made about the triplets. As someone had said, love shouldn't be conditional.

Cole. Cole had said that.

He'd get a kick out of this marble run, she thought, wishing he was here. But she wasn't ready to talk to him. Not until she figured out how she'd gotten so mixed up in the first place.

Sunday afternoon was a good time to solicit her mother's input. Stacy just hoped her father wouldn't hit the roof again.

She called her mom's cell phone. "It's me," she said when Ellen answered.

"Good timing. Your dad's out playing golf."

Her mother had instantly assumed they should keep the conversation secret from her father. Grateful as Stacy was to have her on her side, the reaction made her uneasy. "I was hoping he'd changed his mind."

"Are you all right?" her mom responded. "I've been worried."

"Andrew's wife is leaving him," Stacy burst out with the news. "He cheated on her, too."

"That doesn't surprise me."

"Because he did it once?"

"Because that's the kind of man he was," Ellen said simply.

"Mom, if you knew he was like that, why didn't you say anything?" Stacy demanded. "When I asked you about the perfume on his clothes, you advised me not to hassle him."

"Men are like that." Ellen sounded resigned. "If you pick a fight, you drive them away."

Surely she didn't mean… "You aren't talking about Dad!"

The silence lengthened. Over the phone, Stacy heard a sigh of confirmation.

Around her, the earth seemed to be shifting and the landscape transforming. Suddenly, everything looked different. "That's why you used to act moody sometimes?"

"I'm sorry I made excuses," her mother answered. "I was trying to protect you. It was easier to take the blame myself."

"And let me serve as go-between to patch things up." No wonder Stacy had become the peacemaker in the family. Without realizing what was wrong, she'd had a child's sense of being responsible for grownups' behavior.

"You fell into that role," Ellen admitted.

"And Dad let me fix his mistakes." Grimly, she amended that. "Not mistakes. He didn't stumble and fall into bed with other women."

"Don't be crude, Stacy."

"You're criticizing *me?*"

"No." Her mom seemed to struggle for words. "Your dad does love us, you know."

"Does he?" It wasn't only her marriage that Stacy had failed to see clearly. She'd believed she came from an ideal, loving family, while all along they'd been wildly dysfunctional. "What else am I missing? Come on, Mom. There's more, isn't there?"

"Four years ago, we told you we were moving to Salt Lake to be near Ellie," her mother said slowly.

"But?"

"That wasn't the only reason."

Stacy stopped pacing and sat on the couch. "Go on."

"He'd had a few affairs in the past, but nothing that threatened our marriage," her mother said. "Then I discovered he'd been involved for over a year with a fellow pharmacist. He was keeping some of his clothes at her apartment, and she wanted him to leave me."

"And he has the nerve to pass judgment on my behavior?" Stacy reined in her outrage, determined to hear the whole miserable story. "How did you find out?"

"The woman called to tell me about the affair." From Ellen's shaky tone, Stacy could picture her mom's drawn face. "She assumed I'd throw him out. Instead, I gave him an ultimatum."

"Move to Utah or you'd leave him," Stacy guessed.

Ellen gave a small sniff. "He agreed. He swore he couldn't live without me, that I was the center of his life."

"I must have heard part of that, or maybe you told me about it." Stacy no longer recalled the details, just her reaction. "I thought it was romantic."

"I let you down," Ellen said sadly. "When you married a man a lot like your father, I should have spoken up sooner. I should have protected you, but you were madly in love and I assumed he'd get his act together. First you fell for Andrew, and now you're pregnant by some jerk—"

"No, I'm not," Stacy interrupted. "I mean, he isn't a jerk." Beyond that, she had no desire to discuss Cole. He was so honest and kind and straightforward, he didn't belong in this conversation.

"I shouldn't have mentioned any of this," Ellen said abruptly. "I got carried away because I'm worried about you. Talking about these personal things…it's disloyal to your father."

"My father is disloyal to us," Stacy answered indignantly.

"I hear his car in the driveway," her mom said. "Honey, if you need me, I can come and stay with you for a while."

A kind offer. But Stacy didn't want mothering. "No, thanks."

"We'll talk again soon." Quickly, her mother added, "Don't mention any of this to your sister, all right?"

"Not unless she asks. But you should tell her."

"She married a different sort of guy," Ellen answered. "Luckily. But I'll keep my eyes open."

"Good." After a quick farewell, Stacy hung up.

On the coffee table, the African violet Cole had given her was bursting with tiny blooms against fuzzy, deep green leaves. She'd stuck it there, with the wrong sort of light and without any special food, and yet it was blossoming. She didn't deserve to have such a thriving plant, Stacy thought.

She'd dreamed of a love that transcended the ordinary, of storybook romance and passion. Like Andrew had provided—as a cover for his deceptions.

This had been a weekend for revelations. When the world stopped jolting on its axis, where would it end?

The phone rang. Harper. "Hi," Stacy said.

"I've been trying to get through to you for ten minutes," her friend exclaimed. "You're missing… Oh, wait. It's a video. You can start at the beginning. Is your computer on?"

"Not yet."

"Well, there's something you'd better see."

Chapter Eighteen

No matter how many times Stacy saw Cole on-screen, the sight of him always filled her with pride. He held himself with assurance, yet with none of Andrew's arrogant pride. Cole drew confidence from knowledge and purpose, not egotism.

Stacy relaxed as she watched his image on her laptop, which she'd set up on her bedroom desk. He sat behind a table next to Jennifer Martin's husband, Ian. Cole's stockier build and frank brown eyes gave him a solid air that, in her opinion, overshadowed the blond reporter.

"There is no Daddy Crisis," Cole was saying. "Yes, according to some reports, sperm counts are dropping overall, and we need to figure out why. However, people are reproducing just fine, and I expect they'll continue to do so in the future."

"Doesn't the availability of high-tech assistance ensure that more and more children will inherit lower fertility?" Ian asked.

"In highly developed countries, there may be some slight impact," Cole agreed. "But it isn't anywhere near a crisis."

His next few remarks, recapping familiar material,

faded against the noise that crept back into Stacy's head from her mother's disclosures. Secrets…deception…betrayal. Ellen was still protecting her husband by hiding his misbehavior from their older daughter and by asking Stacy not to confront him about it. That might seem like loyalty, but shielding him from the consequences of his actions only served to enable him.

On the monitor, Cole leaned forward. "We've been discussing facts, but I'm also troubled by the sneering tone of many news reports."

"You've been subjected to a lot of jokes," Ian acknowledged.

"I'm not speaking for myself." Cole's intensity made Stacy quiver. "Patients may be harmed by these slurs on their masculinity. Men with infertility already suffer from anxiety and depression. That can lead to divorce, job loss, sometimes suicide."

The reporter frowned. "I never considered that."

"Men love children just like women do," Cole stated. "For many of us, fatherhood and family become an essential part of our identity."

"Are you referring to yourself now?" Ian zeroed in on his subject. "There's been a lot of publicity about your private life, Dr. Cole."

When Ian's gaze flicked to something off camera, Stacy guessed his wife was signaling him to stop. But the video kept rolling.

"I had three reasons for granting this interview," Cole replied. "First, to clear up this Daddy Crisis nonsense. Second, to advocate for my patients."

"And third?" Ian prompted.

Stacy's hands formed fists. Was he going to mention her? And what would he say if he did?

"It's one thing for the press to poke fun at me professionally," Cole said. "But there's a woman involved here who faces a complicated, potentially dangerous pregnancy. She's turned down my marriage proposal, and since she's much wiser about such things than I am, I presume she's made the right choice."

"I'm not wiser!" Stacy cried, although of course he couldn't hear her.

"She's decided to locate a good—no, great—home for the triplets." Despite a catch in his voice, he hurried on. "The public should respect her choice. I certainly do."

"You're out of the picture?" Ian queried.

"I plan to rededicate myself to helping other couples have *their* children," Cole said. "The medical aspects of the situation drew me to my specialty, but becoming a father, even if I never get to hold my children, has sensitized me at a deeper level. While I hope my future will include marrying and having children, for now, I'll concentrate on treating patients."

"Any final words?" Ian asked.

"I hope the press will quit sensationalizing. They can better serve the public by informing them of scientific facts." Cole's eyes narrowed, and for a moment Stacy expected him to add some further rebuke, but he held back.

"Thank you." The reporter faced the camera. "We've been talking with Dr. Cole Rattigan, head of the men's fertility program at Safe Harbor Medical Center. This is Ian Martin for *On The Prowl in Orange County.* Thanks for watching."

The on-screen window went black. Stacy closed the website and discovered she was trembling.

Despite her reservations, she'd hoped—without acknowledging it—that Cole would make a passionate public statement about how much he loved her. Instead, he sounded as if he'd closed off a chapter in his life and opened a new one. A chapter that didn't include her.

He'd attempted to protect her from the press. Wasn't that what she wanted?

Stacy went into the kitchen and fixed a cup of herbal tea to settle her stomach. Although she'd eaten a late breakfast, pregnancy-inspired hunger pangs sent her foraging through the fridge.

Aside from bread, eggs and a little lettuce, it was nearly bare. However, in the freezer, she found tubs of ice cream.

Not very healthy, but there was less than a quarter of a tub left of rocky road. That meant, according to the unwritten laws of ice cream etiquette, that Stacy could eat it directly out of the carton, which made it irresistible.

Sitting at the table, she savored the mixture of chocolate, mini marshmallows and chopped walnuts. *Cole didn't have to leave these.* He'd taken other food items. Yet despite being kicked out, he'd left this for her to enjoy.

She pictured him in the parking garage, asking her to marry him while he rescued her lipstick from behind a tire. All she'd thought about was how unromantic he was, and she'd assumed that he was proposing out of duty. Now, to her shame, she recalled comparing him mentally to Andrew. Andrew, who covered his selfish nature with elaborate gifts and fancy words.

Dear, sweet Cole had brought her an African violet and a sack of tiramisu, like a child eager to please. He'd fetched take-out food when she was hungry. Rescued her from a mountain of hard-boiled eggs and a pair of unfinished Boston cream pies. Tempted her out of a bad mood with a movie and popcorn. Offered to pay half the rent when she initially refused to let him move in, and later, left quietly despite already having paid. And he'd risked public humiliation by refusing to hide his involvement with her pregnancy.

A song lyric popped into Stacy's mind. She recognized the line from the musical *Fiddler on the Roof.* "If that's not love, what is?"

She buried her face in her hands. How had she missed this? She'd pushed Cole away time and again. But she hadn't really wanted him to go, had she?

Underneath, she'd believed that a man who loved her enough would see past her defenses into her heart. That he'd find the feelings she hid even from herself, and refuse to let her go.

But he had. He'd just stated publicly that he was moving forward, without her. Not a word of criticism, either.

She supposed she could blame her confusion on her parents' screwed-up values. But Cole had been right in front of her, offering everything. And she'd seen only his flaws.

When Stacy lifted her hands, they were wet with tears. This time, there was no Cole to dry them.

It might not be too late. But after what he'd said in the interview, she doubted he would show up here again to comfort her.

She had to let him know that she saw him clearly now. That she wanted him to ask her again to marry him, and that this time, the answer would be yes.

EARLY MONDAY, outside the hospital, Cole found a handful of reporters waiting with the usual array of cameras and microphones. To his satisfaction, the tone of their questions had changed.

They asked about the impact of infertility on men and how this led to depression and suicide. Although he had no statistics—fortunately, in his opinion, since he didn't want to emphasize the negative—he was able to expand on his insights into men's needs and vulnerabilities.

"Fathers are the men who love and protect children, whether or not they provide the sperm," he told the cameras. "They're the ones who are there for you when you fall down or need a helping hand. They're also the ones who stand by Mom, who listen to her and support her."

He didn't mention that his own biological father had done none of those things. True, Jean-Paul Duval had simply been honoring his agreement with Cole's mother, but neither of them had consulted their son.

After Cole excused himself to prepare for surgery, he realized he didn't have to cite his absentee dad in so many words. His aching childhood loneliness informed every word he spoke.

Along the route to his office, several staff members stopped to compliment him on the interview. When he checked his email, he found messages from the administrator, Owen, Adrienne, Zack and several other physicians, cheering him on.

"I never thought I'd say this, but you're an inspiration," Zack had written.

Not exactly an overwhelming compliment, Cole reflected in amusement. Or perhaps it was.

His upbeat mood didn't last long. There was, he saw, no message from Stacy, not that he'd been naive enough to expect one.

Her stopping by on Friday night with the relinquishment papers had brought home her determination to put him and, soon, this pregnancy behind her. Since it would be awkward having her assist him, Cole had emailed the nursing director on Saturday, requesting to switch nurses for his surgeries this week.

All that remained was for him to sign those papers. Yet every time he looked at the legal words that would cut his bond to his children forever, something held him back.

She must be irritated at the delay. Well, he'd get it done this week.

On the surgical board, Cole saw that Anya Meeks had been assigned to him, while Stacy was assisting Zack. Anya didn't know Cole's preferences and lacked Stacy's gift for anticipating which instrument he needed next, but she was learning.

Then he spotted a dearly familiar lady emerging from the elevator. Silky brown curls, a cute, pointy chin and a figure growing lusher by the day… Would he ever get over the twist in his chest at the sight of Stacy?

Cole dodged into the operating suite.

DISMAYED, Stacy took in the schedule. She'd checked the board on Friday, so knew it had been altered.

Her first instinct was to march to Betsy Raditch's office and demand to know why. But she could guess well enough: Cole must have requested it.

He didn't want her in his operating room.

Stacy struggled to breathe through the pain. She forced herself to suck in air and get a grip. If anyone saw her acting unsteady, Betsy might assign her to routine office or desk duty for the rest of the pregnancy.

Stacy loved surgical work. And if she behaved like a professional, Cole might take her back…into his O.R.

What about into his life?

She intended to work on that.

Fathers are the men who love and protect children. His words from the interview had a disturbing habit of lingering in Cole's thoughts during the morning's surgeries, like a melody that refused to quit.

He kept visualizing those precious little shapes on the ultrasound screen. And recalling how Owen's twins had become distinct individuals even at the toddler stage.

Here he stood, reversing a vasectomy so his patient would have a chance to become a biological father. How could Cole give up his own babies?

He craved nuzzling their little necks, and watching them grow up with the same yearning he'd felt to be accepted by his own father. That desperate longing had powered his young self through French lessons and enabled him to pass up buying electronic gadgets to save for a plane ticket.

True, his father had disappointed him. But Cole had survived, strengthened by the awareness that at least he'd tried.

During his last operation before lunch, it occurred to him that Stacy was pushing to choose an adoptive couple much too early. Maybe that meant she was trying to lay her own doubts to rest. Otherwise, why the rush to commit?

His pulse speeding, he decided to talk to her. No matter how much it irked her, he couldn't sign those papers without one final effort.

IN THE LUNCHROOM, Stacy sat with Ned and Harper, well aware that they'd be enjoying a freer and livelier conversation without her there. From a nearby table, she kept hearing snatches of dialogue—"I love how he told them off!" and "He didn't exactly call the press morons, but he might as well have"—that indicated hospital staffers on their lunch break were discussing Cole's interview.

Finally, after a halfhearted discussion of changes to the nurses' locker room trailed into silence, Ned said, "Well, let's stop avoiding the subject. What did you think of Cole's interview?"

"He was brilliant." Stacy stared at her half-eaten sandwich. Even her appetite was failing her today. "Did you notice he got the schedule changed?"

"I noticed." Although Ned worked in Dr. Tartikoff's office, he cruised by the surgical floor frequently to chat with nurses there. And he had an inquisitive nature.

"Are you sure that was Cole's doing?" Harper asked gently.

Ned rolled his eyes. "Who else?"

"He's given up on me," Stacy said.

"Isn't that what you wanted?" Ned prodded. "He said in the interview you turned him down."

"I did, but..." Stacy cut to the chase. "I've been an idiot. The truth is, I don't deserve him."

"Don't be ridiculous," Harper said.

Ned regarded her pensively. "You know, Stacy, you don't have to be perfect to deserve love. Sometimes people just want to give it to you."

She blinked back tears. "That's lucky, because I'm not anywhere near perfect." She'd tried with all her might to do everything right, for her parents, for Andrew, for Una. Still she somehow always came up short.

Maybe that didn't matter.

"I'm sorry I made you cry." Ned placed a hand on her arm.

Stacy threw her arms around him. "Thank you, thank you."

"For what?"

"For telling me that it's okay to act stupid."

Ned returned the hug. "Hey, if you liked that—uh, Stacy, you're completely hideous. What do I get now?"

"A punch in the jaw."

"Try the left side," he said. "I cut the right side shaving."

Stacy broke out laughing. Then she glanced across the room and saw Cole staring at the two of them. Mouth tightening, he gripped his tray and headed in the opposite direction.

Oh, great. She'd messed up again.

SITTING ON THE PATIO, chewing and swallowing food that formed lumps in his stomach, Cole wondered why he'd imagined he could walk up to Stacy in the cafeteria and magically vanquish her objections.

He knew she wasn't in love with Ned, but she acted different with him and her other friends than she did with Cole. He'd never been good with people. "Emotionally tone deaf" was how a former coworker had described him. "Somewhere to the right of the autism spectrum" had been Felicia's biased conclusion.

Yet since his involvement with Stacy, he'd gotten to know Zack and Owen on a personal level. He'd fixed food for a housewarming party, and helped Adrienne plant her garden. He'd babysat Mia, all by himself.

Because of Stacy, Cole had formed connections. He would forever be grateful for the vistas she'd opened up, he reflected, staring into a container of chocolate milk.

Too bad she'd broken his heart in the process.

COLE HAD RETREATED onto the patio, Stacy noted as she set her tray on the conveyer belt. Although tempted to scoot out after him, she was keenly aware of the interested gazes of practically everyone in the cafeteria.

Besides, what could she say, other than that she'd been an idiot? A simple "I love you" might do the trick. But it didn't feel like enough.

Despite all she'd learned in the past few days, Stacy still believed that people in love ought to be swept away. That the decision to launch a life together should start with a brass band, speeches and a bottle of champagne smashing across the hull of a ship. Or a reasonable equivalent.

Besides, she had another surgery to prepare for. Aching for the solitary man sitting outside alone, Stacy forced herself to walk away.

Chapter Nineteen

Since he relied on a digital calendar, by late June Cole had long ago thrown out the free paper calendars that came in the mail or were dropped on his desk by pharmaceutical reps. Even online, he couldn't find one with photos of gardens—or better yet, babies—and settled for a site that allowed him to print out pages for each month through the beginning of next year. They might not look like much, but they added a touch of personality to his tiny suite.

Most likely Stacy would deliver early, given the potential complications of bearing triplets. Still, Cole circled her due date in February.

During the evenings that week, he filled in details of how her pregnancy was likely to progress. Presently, at week nine—calculated from the first day of her last period—a typical baby was about an inch long, able to bring its tiny hands together over its heart.

The tenth week would mark the end of the embryonic phase and the start of the fetal period. Rapid growth would double the baby's length by week eleven, with fingernails developing. At week twelve, most likely Stacy's morning sickness would begin to ease. Of course, with triplets, things might be different.

All the while, Cole recognized that this was an exercise in futility. Each day since Monday, he'd meant to sign the relinquishment form and put Stacy's mind to rest. He hadn't forgotten his intention of talking to her first, but once he did, he'd have no excuse to delay further. And he wasn't ready to abandon all hope.

At the hospital, she kept her distance, except for glancing at him nervously once in a while. Her attitude seemed to be catching. On Friday, although Stacy wasn't present in the O.R., Cole noticed sideways glances between the nurses, the anesthesiologist and the urologist, one of the hospital's new fellows, who was assisting him. But when he looked at them directly, each pair of eyes was quickly averted.

Did this mean the press was again pushing some scandal? After a flurry of reports about male suicides, reporters had stopped mentioning Cole. Could his colleagues have heard something he'd missed?

He'd be just as happy to go on missing it. For now, he ignored their irritating behavior.

Later, while cleaning up, he saw that Rod was wearing a red T-shirt under his surgical scrubs. No big deal, except that, seen from the rear, the assisting urologist wore what appeared to be an identical one.

Cole performed a quick mental check. Late June didn't contain any red-themed holidays as far as he knew. No Valentine's Day, no red, white and blue Fourth of July, no Christmas.

"What did you guys do, call each other this morning and coordinate your wardrobes?" he asked.

Rod peered over his shoulder, without turning. "Cracking jokes now, Doc?"

"Forget it." What did he care if the guys dressed alike?

When Cole stepped out of the room, he narrowly avoided a collision with the circulating nurse, who also wore a red T-shirt. At an angle, he saw bold white lettering on the front. Before he could read the words, she folded her arms across her chest.

"I wasn't staring at…" He didn't care to finish that sentence.

"Sure you weren't." She grinned, apparently unoffended.

Down the hall came Zack Sargent, presumably done with his surgery. He'd buttoned his white coat, but there was a patch of red at the throat.

"I must have missed the memo," Cole told him.

"Beg pardon?"

"It seems to be red T-shirt day."

"Oh, that memo." He paused but didn't explain. "So, how's it going?"

"How's what going?" Cole asked.

Down the hall, the elevator doors opened and Owen emerged. He was wearing something red under his coat, too.

Cole could have kicked himself for failing to sift through his email before heading into surgery. He'd lingered too long over breakfast, jumping up to make notes on the calendar pages for July and August.

Wait a minute. Harper was coming from the stairs, with red under her blue-flowered uniform. What was she doing here? She worked in the medical office building.

Everyone was gathering in the hall, as if waiting for something. Cole decided to wait, too.

The elevator opened again, releasing Ned and Lucky. Both had red T-shirts peeking from beneath their navy uniforms. “Et tu, Brute?” Cole asked, dismayed that his nurse hadn’t let him in on the secret.

“Where’s Stacy?” Lucky responded. “Oh, good, here she comes.”

Around the corner, her sweet face flushed, came Stacy. She wore something white, not red, under the V-neck of her light blue scrubs. Maybe she hadn’t read the memo, either.

“Gang’s all here,” Ned called.

“Okay,” Cole said, “what’s the joke?”

As if at a signal—if there was one, he missed it—the people around him pulled back their jackets to reveal white lettering on red fabric. The T-shirts all said the same thing: Will You Marry Me?

“Is this some weird California ritual?” Cole asked.

Then he realized Stacy was pulling off her light blue top to reveal her white T-shirt. In red letters it asked Will You Marry Me?

“What’s going on?” Cole inquired.

“I’m proposing,” she said.

No one moved. From down the hall, he heard the wheels of a gurney rolling along. Other than that, silence reigned.

“To me?” he asked.

Rod rolled his eyes. “You better say yes before somebody else takes her up on it.”

Cole swallowed, desperately hoping this was real. He felt as if he should do something grand in return, like go down on one knee and produce a ring, except he hadn’t bought one.

“You don’t have to say yes,” Stacy murmured.

That was it, the word he sought. “Yes!” he shouted, so loudly the circulating nurse gave a startled jump, and Lucky blinked in surprise.

"Did anyone *not* hear that?" Owen queried ironically.

"Yes!" Cole repeated. "I love you!"

"I love you, too," Stacy choked out.

To hell with what people thought. Cole lunged over, scooped her into his arms and kissed her. She melted against him, kissing him back. It felt wonderful.

From behind, he heard people clapping. "Why don't you guys go eat lunch?" he called, casting a meaningful glare in their direction.

"You can keep the T-shirts," Stacy added.

"I'm saving mine for April Fool's Day," Ned joked.

"I'm saving mine for Halloween." Rod waggled his eyebrows.

They scuttled off, by stairs and by elevator, and for all Cole cared, by emergency exit and rope-and-ladder.

"Oh, sweetheart." He refused to let go, afraid that if he did, Stacy might disappear and he'd wake up. He'd had a very vivid dream about her once before, and the result had been triplets. He doubted he'd get that lucky again.

She nestled against him. "Please forgive me for turning you down in the first place. You're a magnificent man and I can't wait to spend the rest of my life with you."

"Does this mean I can move back in?" Cole chuckled at his own question. "I guess that's kind of a given, huh?"

Arms looped around his shoulders, Stacy tapped her forehead against his. "Take as much time as you need to let this sink in."

She understood him, Cole thought in wonder. She accepted that he needed a few minutes to digest the breathtaking fact that they were engaged. "We are keeping the babies, right?" Another foolish question, but she'd been so determined to relinquish them.

Stacy smiled. "I told you once that there was a couple who were meant to have these children. I finally figured out who it is."

"Us?" he asked hopefully.

"You got it."

"We can buy a house where they'll have room to play," Cole ventured. "Or would you rather we spent the money on a big wedding?"

"Small wedding, big house," Stacy affirmed.

"I'm glad." He'd look for one with space for a garden as well as a play area.

They were drawing curious glances from passing staff members and a patient on a gurney, en route to surgery.

With a sigh, Stacy released him. "You can move your furniture in this weekend. And you're staying over with me tonight, okay?"

"You bet." An idea occurred to him. "Is it all right if I put something up on your wall? I started a countdown calendar for the triplets."

"What a great idea." She laced her fingers through his. "You're amazing."

"I hope you mean that in a good way." He'd been called amazing before in a variety of contexts, not all flattering.

"Absolutely," Stacy said. "Let's have lunch. Our kids are starving and so am I."

"Did I tell you about eating dinner with Owen and the twins?" Cole asked as they strolled hand in hand toward the elevator. "They do funny things with their food."

"I can't wait to hear all about it," she answered, laughing.

He wasn't sure what he'd said to amuse her, but it didn't matter. Because Stacy loved him just as he was, and Cole planned on spending the rest of his life making her happy.

HE'D NEVER SLEPT IN Stacy's bed before, Cole realized as he eased between the sheets in his crisp pajamas. He loved the lily fragrance and silky texture of the sheets—and the sight of Stacy's body in a filmy nightgown, silhouetted against the light from the bathroom.

"I always think it's a shame to save the wedding night for after the wedding," she teased as she joined him in bed.

"We didn't," he pointed out.

"I keep forgetting how literal-minded you are." Snuggling against him, she kissed the hollow beneath his jaw.

Joyously, Cole rolled onto his side, stroking her hip and waist. When his hand cupped her breast, she gasped.

He waited a second, to make sure she wasn't objecting, and bent to kiss the tight nub. Her sigh of pleasure tightened his body, making him hard and eager.

Cole wished he was a more skilled lover. Fortunately, Stacy didn't hesitate to show him what she liked—long caresses, gentle kisses, his bare body exploring and arousing hers.

When he slid inside her, he felt bathed in a glow, as if all his cells were lightly shivering. Every movement simmered through him, and it wasn't nearly long enough before he lost control, moving harder and faster, urged on by Stacy's moans.

For a glorious instant, they fused, vibrating at exactly the same frequency. The feeling ebbed slowly, leaving him with a sense of peace and belonging.

"Was that…?" He didn't know how to finish the sentence.

"Even better," Stacy murmured.

"How soon can we get married?" While Cole didn't believe she'd change her mind, he wasn't taking any chances.

"How about September?" she asked.

"Any particular reason?"

"The weather's usually good." She shrugged.

"This is Southern California. The weather's always good," he pointed out.

She kissed his shoulder. "And I should still be able to walk down the aisle."

Cole recalled his image of rolling her down the aisle in a bridal gown with her feet propped up. "That's a good reason."

Stacy didn't seem to want to talk anymore. That was fine with him.

There'd be plenty of time to make plans. All the time in the world.

BY SUNDAY EVENING, Cole had moved his furniture back in, although he still shared Stacy's bed. Every time she touched his hair or felt his warmth against her, she reveled in the magic that had caught her unawares. That old cliché about looking for love in all the wrong places…if only she'd listened, she could have had this sooner.

His printed-out calendar, tacked neatly on the wall in the kitchen, told the story of the children growing inside her. While he washed the dinner dishes, Stacy studied the entries, one hand over her abdomen.

Cole had incredibly neat handwriting. Everything about him was orderly and reliable. Yet there was nothing stodgy about the joy on his face when he looked at her.

How incredible that this had happened.

When the phone summoned her, Stacy scooped it from her pocket. It was Ellen. Guiltily, she reflected that she hadn't called her mother yet. She'd been engaged for two entire days and she had no excuse for not notifying her parents, except that her feelings for them were complicated.

She'd better get it over with. "Hi, Mom."

"It's been a week since I heard from you," Ellen said. "Are you okay?"

"Cole and I are getting married." So much for subtlety. "Mom, I can't wait for you to meet him! Well, I guess you've seen him on the news. He's so wonderful."

Stepping out of the kitchen, Cole gave a pleased wave. He didn't take the phone to introduce himself, though. Stacy was glad. She'd prefer to prepare her fiancé before he chatted with his future in-laws.

He disappeared into the kitchen.

"I hope you aren't doing this just to satisfy your father," Ellen said.

"Not at all." Had her mom missed the part about how fabulous Cole was? "We love each other. It's perfect."

"You may be idealizing," she warned.

"In this case, it's justified."

"Uh-oh." Her mother lowered her voice to a whisper. "Your dad just came in. He went for a walk after dinner, and usually he's gone at least half an hour. I thought it was safe to call." In the background, Stacy heard him ask who it was.

"Tell him, Mom," she said.

"It's Stacy." Ellen's voice grew fainter as she addressed her husband. "She's engaged."

"This isn't one of those engagements that lasts for years, is it?" he grumbled in the background.

"Put him on," Stacy insisted.

"Maybe you should..." Whatever her mother meant to say, she didn't finish. Instead, random noises indicated the phone was changing hands.

"Stacy?" her father said. "Congratulations. I'm glad you came to your senses."

A burst of anger nearly sent her into attack mode. She curbed it, not for his sake but for hers and her mom's. "My senses have nothing to do with it. I'm marrying the man I love. Not for you, Dad. Not for anyone else. For me."

From the kitchen, a series of bangs and a delicious buttery scent indicated Cole was making popcorn. Suddenly Stacy wasn't angry at her father anymore. Only sad for him and her mom, who could have had so much more happiness over the years if he'd truly devoted himself to their marriage.

"I'd like to walk you down the aisle." Was that a note of uncertainty?

"Of course," Stacy said. "And Dad..." If she chewed him out, it might gratify her sense of justice, but Ellen had revealed his transgressions in confidence. Besides, Stacy loved her father. "I was lucky to find a man who'll be a great husband. Who puts me and the kids first. Who'll always be there for us. When you meet him, you'll understand."

"He sounds like a terrific fellow," Al said. "I'm glad

for you, baby. Please forgive me for what I said last time. I love you."

"I love you, too." Stacy was tempted to say more, but had no wish to stir up trouble. "Take care of Mom, will you?"

"Sure."

"I mean that."

"What's she been telling you?" he asked.

"Nothing that I can't see for myself," Stacy said. "I've learned a lot from Cole about how actions speak louder than words."

There was a long pause.

"You shouldn't take the people you love for granted," she added. "They might not always be there."

Then he said something that surprised her. "Your mother's been urging me to go away with her for a marriage renewal weekend. Maybe that's not such a bad idea."

"It gets my vote," Stacy told him.

"Might even be fun," he said. "I'm pleased for you, honey. I'm sure you've picked the right man this time."

"You'd better believe it."

After saying goodbye to her mother, Stacy finished the call. She was happy that her father had agreed to invest more in his marriage. In their sixties, her parents might have another twenty or more years together.

Cole walked in with a large bowl of popcorn. "Everything shipshape on the home front?"

She related the conversation. "They'll have to negotiate their own peace from now on. I'm resigning from that role."

"Maybe we should go on one of those marriage weekends." After setting the bowl on the coffee table, Cole retrieved some DVDs from a cabinet.

"I believe you have to be married first."

"Minor impediment. But it can wait." He helped her onto the couch as if she was already ballooning. "While we're on the subject, I thought we might watch a movie about weddings, to get ideas."

"Oh, fun!" She studied the DVD choices. *The Runaway Bride, Four Weddings and a Funeral* and *Bride and Prejudice*. "What's that one?"

"It's the Bollywood version of Jane Austen's novel," he explained. "Lots of catchy singing and dancing in India."

"You're kidding."

"It's one of my favorites."

"I'll try it." He was right, she discovered. The classic story translated beautifully into another culture, with the bonus of upbeat melodies and appealing performers.

Afterward, they watched the outtakes, which were hilarious. Her head on Cole's shoulder, Stacy murmured, "Do you realize we have to choose three baby names?"

"Six," he corrected. "Since we don't know the gender yet."

"We could pick unisex names," she said. "Or wait."

"Why play it safe?" Cole said.

"Yes, let's live dangerously." As long as they were being silly, she added, "I know! I'll pick the girls' names and you can pick the boys' names."

"How about Harpo, Chico and Groucho?"

"Never mind," Stacy said. "I'll pick all the names."

"Okay." Cole's arm tightened around her. "Want me to get up and put on another movie?"

"Maybe later." Stacy preferred to treasure their quiet intimacy awhile longer. To bask in the fact that she was living a love story of her own, complete with a happy ending. No doubt they'd commit more bloopers along the way, but sometimes that was the best part.

Or rather, with Cole in her arms, it was *all* the best part.

* * * * *

Watch for Jacqueline Diamond's next book in the Safe Harbor Medical series, HIS BABY DREAM, *coming June 2013, only from Harlequin American Romance!*

COMING NEXT MONTH
from Harlequin® American Romance®

AVAILABLE APRIL 2, 2013

#1445 HIS CALLAHAN BRIDE'S BABY

Callahan Cowboys

Tina Leonard

Sweet and independent Taylor Waters won't accept Falcon Callahan's marriage proposal. But he's determined to win Diablo's best girl, even when the whole town puts him to the test!

#1446 HER COWBOY DILEMMA

Coffee Creek, Montana

C.J. Carmichael

Prodigal daughter Cassidy Lambert is home—temporarily—to help out at the family ranch. But seeing local vet Dan Farley again is making her question her decision to live in the big city.

#1447 NO ORDINARY COWBOY

Rodeo Rebels

Marin Thomas

Lucy Durango needs Tony Bravo to teach her how to ride bulls. Tony reluctantly agrees, and he'll do what he can to keep her safe. Even if her daddy warns him to stay away....

#1448 THE RANCHER AND THE VET

Fatherhood

Julie Benson

Reed Montgomery returns to the family ranch in Colorado to care for his fourteen-year-old niece, Jess. There Reed must face his difficult past, his cowboy roots and Avery McAlister, the girl he loved and left.

The CALLAHAN COWBOY *series continues with Tina Leonard's HIS CALLAHAN BRIDE'S BABY.*

Falcon has his work cut out for him trying to convince Taylor to be his wife—but if his proposal doesn't work, he'll lose his ranch land to his siblings!

Taylor Waters was one of Diablo's "best" girls. She had a reputation for being wild at heart. Untamable. Men threw themselves at her feet and she walked all over them with a sweet-natured smile.

Falcon Chacon Callahan studied the well-built brunette behind the counter of Banger's Bait and Tackle diner. He'd talked the owner, Jillian, into selling him one last beer, even though the diner usually closed at the stroke of midnight on the weekends. It was his Saturday night off from Rancho Diablo, and he hadn't wanted to do anything but relax and consider what he was going to do with his life once his job at the ranch was over.

Taylor was more of an immediate interest. She smiled that cute pixie smile at him and Falcon sipped his beer, deciding on a whim—some might call it a hunch—to toss his heart into the Taylor tizzy. "I need a wife," he said.

"So I hear. So we all hear." She came and sat on the bar stool next to him. "You'll get it figured out eventually, Falcon."

"Marry me, Taylor."

"I know you're not drunk enough to propose, Falcon. You're just crazy, like we've always heard." She smiled so adorably, all of the sting fled her words. In fact, she was so cute about her opinion that Falcon felt his chest expand.

"I leave crazy to my brothers. My sister is the wild and crazy one. Me, I'm somewhere on the other side of the

HAREXP0413

spectrum." He leaned over and kissed her lightly on the lips. Falcon grinned. "What's your answer, cupcake?"

"You're not serious." Taylor shook her head. "I've known you for over a year. Of all the Callahans, you're the one the town's got odds on being last to the altar." She got up and sashayed to the register. His eyes followed her movements hungrily. "A girl would be a fool to fall for you, Falcon Callahan."

That did not sound like a *yes.*

But Falcon is a cowboy who always gets his way! Watch for his story coming in April 2013, only from Harlequin® American Romance®.

HAREXP0413